BLUES FOR A LOST CHILDHOOD

by Antônio Torres and available
from Readers International:

The Land

ANTÔNIO TORRES

BLUES
FOR A LOST CHILDHOOD
A Novel of Brazil

Translated with an Introduction
by
John Parker

readers international

The title of this book in Portuguese is *Balada da infância perdida,* first published in 1986 by Editora Nova Fronteira S.A., Botafogo, Rio de Janeiro.
© Antônio Torres 1986

First published in English by Readers International Inc, Columbia, Louisiana and Readers International, London. Editorial inquiries to the London office at 8 Strathray Gardens, London NW3 4NY, England. US/Canadian inquiries to the Subscriber Service Department, P.O. Box 959, Columbia LA 71418-0959 USA.

Translation © Readers International Inc 1989

Cover illustration by Hildebrando de Castro, Rio de Janeiro
Cover design by Jan Brychta
Printed and bound in Malta by Interprint Limited

Library of Congress Catalog Card Number: 89-61872

British Library Cataloguing in Publication Data
Torres, Antônio, *1940-*
    Blues for a lost childhood: a novel of Brazil.
    I. Title [Balada da infância perdida. *English*]
    869.3[F]

ISBN 0-930523-67-9 Hardcover
ISBN 0-930523-68-7 Paperback

Antônio Torres:
Protesting Underdevelopment

Introduction
by John Parker

"And suddenly I realised I was a writer, and that I was not alone. We were a whole generation in the seventies, up and down the country, writing and discussing our literature; and a new awareness grew of our national and regional strengths." - Antônio Torres

Born in a small town in the dusty interior of the state of Bahia, the author of *Blues for a Lost Childhood* made the trek to the industrial south, like so many northeasterners before and since. He didn't, it is true, have to suffer the 1500-mile journey clinging to the shafts of a rickety truck known as a *pau-de-arara* (parrot's perch). He was literate and articulate; he had been a journalist in the state capital, Salvador; he went on to work on newspapers in São Paulo and Rio, before moving into the heady, precarious world of advertising evoked in his latest novel. However, unlike the book's nameless narrator, to whom he has clearly given some of his own situational traits, Torres' concern with his native Northeast does not stop at nostalgia for its alcoholic pleasures. Rather, he can be seen as a spokesman for those poor migrants, symbolic of Brazil's underdevelopment, of the cleavage between the 'two Brazils', north and south, and in the north itself between the handful of urban centres and the vast hinterland controlled by landowners recalcitrant to all attempts at agrarian reform.

This had been the subject matter of the so-called 'novel of the Northeast', in the 1930s, when writers such as Jorge Amado, Graciliano Ramos and Rachel de Queiroz attacked the social evils of the areas to which they belonged. Their writing used descriptive realism to depict the lives of poor estate workers, debt labourers, sharecroppers, cowboys and their families, beset by the crushing problems of an unjust social system, frequently made worse by hostile climatic conditions, for which there was no solution other than migration to the growing cities of the south. Antônio Torres sees his generation as heir to the ethical position of Amado, Ramos and others, in facing and questioning Brazil's most pressing national problems, bridging the gap with the thirties after a lengthy period during which the majority of writers had turned their attention to the psychological concerns of the individual and to experimenting with the aesthetic claims of fictional form. *Os subterrâneos da liberdade* (Freedom Underground), Jorge Amado's socialist-realist fresco of communist party activity during the early years of the Estado Novo, was the last major work in the socio-political line followed by the Northeastern novelists. However, appearing in 1954, the year of President Getúlio Vargas's suicide, it was soon overtaken by Guimarães Rosa's masterpieces, *Grande sertão: Veredas* (*The Devil to Pay in the Backlands*, 1963) and *Corpo de Baile* (Corps de Ballet), both published in 1956, the year which many Brazilian critics have come to consider a watershed which established the 'new fiction'. The political and economic climate was favourable to the aesthetic changes: democratization was followed by the industrial development program of Juscelino Kubitschek, which encouraged hope in a better future, symbolized by the founding of the new capital, Brasilia.

Brazil moved into the era of *bossa nova* and the world football championship, both sources of international recognition, while in the Northeast things began to move, with the formation of the Peasant Leagues and, when the great drought of 1958 claimed Kubitschek's attention, the creation of Sudene, a government agency, to plan and finance development in the region. Fiction, for the most part, responded more to industrial development in the south, rejecting the perceived threat of massification, in the name of the individual identity and of creating a literature in form and content accessible only to an educated elite.

The 1964 military coup accentuated this tendency, particularly from 1968, when the regime, under Medici, entered its most violently repressive phase and literary reference, when it exists, became oblique, opaquely allegorical, its meaning to be teased out by inference. José J.Veiga uses Orwellian fable (*A hora dos ruminantes,* 1966; *The Three Trials of Manirema,* 1970) and fantastic realism (*A máquina extraviada,* 1968; *The Misplaced Machine & Other Stories,* 1970) to convey a threatening atmosphere of oppression; in *Sombras de reis barbudos,* 1972 (Shadows of Bearded Kings), the oppression is openly aggressive and all-embracing, but the writing continues to be dominated by the fantastic. The regime's censors could hardly identify the source of oppression with the military government, without admitting precisely what Brazilian official propaganda was doing its best to deny to its supporters in the western democracies!

For Antônio Torres and most of the writers he recognizes as belonging to his generation, such was the type of national fiction they read and discussed in their late teens and early twenties, as they too began to appear in print: a fiction that was (ostensibly) apolitical, individualistic or universalizing, metaphysical, mythopoeic, divorced from immediate or identifiable reality, concerned with formal innovation (disruption of linear narrative, use of stream of consciousness, multiple narrators, etc.), all part of a general move away from the traditions of bourgeois realism. The short story, too, had begun to acquire more importance, in the hands of Rosa, Clarice Lispector, Dourado, Veiga and others, who experimented with new techniques, creating strange atmospheres, using children or abnormal characters to produce 'defamiliarization' effects. The younger generation followed their example, and in the late sixties and early seventies we find them forming groups and founding magazines to serve as outlets for their work and to attract the attention of their contemporaries. Their fiction is seldom overtly political, but if a word to the wise is sufficient one can be sure that the Brazilian context would promote certain interpretations, particularly among the student body, which never ceased its hostility to the regime. Seen in this light, the attitude of the jury member (Luiz Vilela, 'Júri', 1967) who, revolted by the attitudes of everyone in court, decides he will vote against the sentence, regardless of the accused's guilt, acquires a clear political dimension. Another story by Vilela, 'O buraco' ('The hole'), in which the narrator starts digging a hole as a child and ends up isolating himself inside it, transformed into an armadillo, can be seen as an allegory of man's alienation in modern industrial societies, but going underground suggests another meaning in what was rapidly becoming a police state.

Vilela's novel *Os novos* (1971, The Young Ones) skates sufficiently close to subversion to give credence to such interpretations. Subversion is present, too, in Oswaldo França Júnior's first novel, *O viúvo* (1965, The Widower), in the upbringing the bereaved narrator gives to his children, intended to instill in them a sturdy independence and self-reliance, against all the attempts at interference by traditional family authority. In *Um dia no Rio* (1969, One Day in Rio), França's central character, accidentally caught up in a running battle between students and riot police in central Rio, pronounces no judgment, but his eyes and ears serve as the filter for the expression of popular anger. We shall, however, look in vain for further direct reference to political events in the work of this author, until 1984, when he eventually confronted his own forced retirement from the air force, twenty years previously, in a novel (*O passo-bandeira*) which points to the paranoid authoritarianism of the regime, but seems not to question its legitimacy and avoids addressing its cruel repression of elementary human rights.

The most overtly political novelist of the period must be Antônio Callado, an already established writer and journalist, whose books in this phase revolve around urban guerrilla activity (*Bar Don Juan,* 1971; *Reflexos do baile,* 1976, Reflections of the Dance). That they were allowed to circulate may be explained by the lyrical incapacity of the would-be guerrillas, in the first, and the hopelessness of their task, in the second, crushed by a merciless machine: perhaps the censors weighed this indication of the regime's invincibility favourably against the crude detailing of torture in the second novel, which went through four editions within months of publication. Torture features also in one section of Sergio Sant'Anna's *Confissões de Ralfo* (1975, Ralph's Confessions), a satirical carnavalesque parody of contemporary bourgeois civilisation subtitled 'An imaginary autobiography', which proclaims its literariness sufficiently often to divert suspicion.

Yet all this fiction (of which I have mentioned only a fraction) is essentially middle-class. Even when it seems to confront the regime, it concerns middle-class individuals, as Sant'Anna reminds us, through a character in a more recent work. In this respect, it seems to me that Antônio Torres adds a dimension precisely because, from his first novel, *Um cão uivando para a lua* (1972, A Hound Baying at the Moon), he turns his attention to the disinherited. Like the author, the central character migrated from Bahia to become a journalist in São Paulo and from there went on to work in advertising in Rio. The novel consists largely of the weaving together of his recollections of scenes of misery and exploitation, of police coercion, of poverty and backwardness, of official corruption and inhumanity, which drove him to mental collapse and internment in a sanatorium. This is where we find him at the beginning of the novel, and it provides the one fixed point for the narrative fragments, in much the same way as do the drunken nightmares in *Blues for a Lost Childhood,* Virinha's dreams in *Adeus, velho* (1981, Goodbye, Old Man) and Gil's reconstruction of past events as he lies dying, in *Carta ao bispo* (1979, Letter to the Bishop). Rejecting the traditional linear plot, Torres deliberately restructures chronological time to create a kaleidoscopic vision and achieves a cumulative effect by introducing the exemplary stories of many individuals without the need for secondary plots. In this way, a conversation with a bootblack or with a taxi-driver, for instance, or items supposedly encountered in a newspaper, can be inserted almost anywhere in the text and serve the purpose of denouncing social, economic and political ills in an apparently documentary - and unbiased - fashion.

Another feature of the author's writing is the tendency to share the narrative consciousness between two or more characters. This is particularly the case in *Essa terra* (1976, published in English as *The Land,* 1987) and *Adeus, velho,* which describe the break up of the traditional Northeastern family, when the children reject their elders' unquestioning acceptance of the ideological values enshrined in the region's unchanging social and economic conditions, and attempt to break out of the vicious circle by leaving home in search of something different. What they find, in the great urban centres (Rio, São Paulo, Salvador) may offer advancement, but when achieved, it is precarious and is at the cost of those personal, humane values which the author locates emotionally, against his better reason, in the Northeast of his childhood. This loss, viewed as a quality of the Brazilian character which the military regime has destroyed, constitutes the starting point of *Blues,* represented more concretely by the little blue coffins - the coffins of young children ('angels') - which appear first to the narrator. It also explains the appearance of García Lorca and the quotation of the opening lines of his 'Balada de la placeta', as well as the greater abundance in this novel of quoted verses and songs, and might be responsible for the episode of the magic battle tank. Torres cites popular, oral literature as a major influence in his writing (the episode of the famous bandit Lampião in hell is not his invention) and this would offer a further explanation, not only for the many quotations, but for the intertextual weaving of phrases, or whole lines, from poems and songs, into the body of the text: the "splendid cradle", for instance, comes from the Brazilian national anthem, as does "days of yore", an obvious anachronism in the novel's characteristically colloquial style.

Blues for a Lost Childhood covers, in its syncopated temporal arrangement, a period of some thirty years if we situate Calunga's first appearance in early adolescence, well before the 1964 coup, by which time he is a grown man; and his younger cousin, our narrator, has by then lost his first job in São Paulo. Calunga's participation in the Bahia-Brasilia march would be in the Kubitschek period, while Marshal Lott was an unsuccessful presidential candidate in 1960. Calunga's communist sympathies during this phase would correspond to the leftward swing in national politics under the presidency of Goulart. After the coup, when the narrator, in retrospective fantasy (the magic tank episode), points up United States involvement and Calunga 'goes on strike', we accompany the political scene indirectly through the analogy of Calunga's decline. It should be mentioned that the name formed from the first syllables of the character's full name is no accident, being a Brazilian word meaning, among other things: a minor African deity and its fetish; runt; mouse; doll; a human figure as drawn by a child; any insignificant thing or person; a trucker's assistant. Perhaps a way of insinuating that, despite his qualities, Calunga didn't have a chance, because of his socio-cultural inheritance; or, maybe, that his supreme quality, in his creator's eyes, his refusal to make concessions to the extreme form of capitalism imposed on a developing nation by its own armed forces on behalf of foreign masters, inevitably led to his being crushed and forced back to his native Bahia to die. The narrator, who has made the concessions to the system, lives in daily fear of losing his job and is subject to the sort of nightmare which the novel has narrated. As for the author, it may be that Junco (his birthplace) is now only a spot on the map, but even now, in the words of the poet Carlos Drummond de Andrade, "como dói" (how it aches).

Aveiro, Portugal
July 1989

BLUES FOR A LOST CHILDHOOD

"What's that supposed to be?" the severe man asked me indignantly.

"It's transitional poetry, war poetry, shock poetry...."

But is there nothing worth saving in all of this? Of course there is! There is a new world filtering through the war's open vents.

- Oswald de Andrade

1

Black-faced ox,
ox with the black face,
come and fetch this baby
who's afraid of
nasty faces.

A lullaby. That's exactly what I need to hear right now.

Sleep, baby, sleep,
night is here and
daddy's coming soon...

My father didn't come and never will. He hates all cities, regardless of size, geographical location, per capita income or population density. He says they are the work of the devil. They have taken all his children from him.

Of course he's not a man of this world. Nor of this time.

He preferred the loneliness of the *caatinga* to the congestion of the building industry.

Yet I know he would be capable of an extreme sacrifice, perhaps the last he would ever make, if I sent him an air ticket with an urgent message:

"I'm dying."

Then he would arrive, with the planks, his tools, the black cloth and other accessories. He would ask for a bottle of rum and get down to work, the way he always did: in silence. That way he would pay me his one and only real tribute.

Maybe he'd be thinking:

"I haven't done them all yet, but I've done a good few already. Won't hurt me to do another."

My father. Poppa. The old boy.

He'll never come to lull me to sleep, the way he did once, long, long ago.

It was one of those sunsets that paint the sky crimson.

And it was the end of another day's work.

It was time to stop for a smoke and a chat.

And there was a mound of hulled beans drawing the men together.

Father lit his cigarette. He looked happy. It was going to be a great year. And you didn't need to have read Confucius or any other Chinese to know that his happiness came from his belly. What were my father and the other workers talking about in that blessed sunset? To remember that now would be expecting too much of a memory soaked in alcohol and wormeaten with folly. All that remains is the recollection of a sort of babble, a certain harmony, the distant sound of tired men's voices - the murmur of a breeze in that far-off eventide.

Perhaps a lullaby, light and tender as the wind falling with the onset of night. A reassuring breeze: everything was hunky-dory. And those voices and that breeze lulled me to sleep lying on the mound of beans. After that I went on sleeping, straddling my father's neck and strapped to his hat, as he walked in the moonlight, carrying me home, to dreamland.

That man is as far away as that time. And he is doubtless still alive and well preserved - in spirits. And, to judge from the hour, he'll still be asleep, and I would give anything to know what he's dreaming about. The wife God carried off centuries ago, amen? The children swept away in life's torrent? Even so, I could swear he does dream. My father. Poppa. The old boy: alone and forgotten in the silence of a hovel, stuck in a futureless gully. Even so. That way his dreams are still scented with the sweet smell of rosemary, while I, reeking with alcohol from every pore, twist and turn in my bed, counting wee blue coffins. With no mother or father to sing me a lullaby.

The lullaby I'm hearing now is quite different.

Piercing squeals and howls, the whirring of helicopters and shouts and panic and dread under a hail of gunfire up in the slum right by my bedside.

And poppa will never come and haul me onto his shoulders and carry me around until I go to sleep.

And Momma's dead already, as I said. The old

wretch.

It's the war: when a child is crying and there's no father to see.

I know it's like that, because nearly every night I see a war, on television.

The same helicopters, the same shooting, the same pandemonium, the same hullabaloo. The same wailing and weeping.

You watch from an armchair, glass in one hand and cigarette in the other.

Afterwards you switch off and go to sleep, oh so good, to sleep, don't remind me of something so good. SLE-EEP.

And dream about an old man, a horse, a dog and a bottle of hooch.

My father.

He'll never come. He never set foot in an airplane.

More chance of my mother's soul coming, she's part of the ether already and, like in a fairy-tale, she's queen of space and flies higher than a falcon.

Lost souls, wandering creatures: come to me. You have nothing to lose. You are masters of your own time.

The worst is, a relative never comes alone.

My mother will be accompanied by my Aunt Madalena, her good sister. The kindly soul who brought me up for a time. And heaven knows how many hangers-on.

Like the kind soul she is, Aunt Madalena will not play hard to get. She will collect her dues. I mean to say the dividends due her kindness, the interest on her past magnanimity.

"You didn't even go to my son's funeral, your cousin he was, as a matter of fact he was a real brother to you. You never so much as had a mass said for him, most likely you don't even remember the day he died nor where he's buried. You never put a single flower on my grave. Perhaps you don't even know that I'm dead."

Come off it, Auntie. Your son Calunga was very close to me, it's true. But I didn't have the physique to keep up with him when it came to drinking. Then he disappeared. And I lost track of him. Died, did he? You don't say. How awful. I liked him a lot. Sincerely. And you've passed on as well? It's too much. Everybody I like is dying. But Calunga, oh hell. He'd be in his forties, wouldn't he? Poor devil. Too much booze. A guy has to be able to take a breather from time to time, don't he?

"And you're going the same way. You're getting to be just like your cousin."

Just like I said. Opening your door and your heart to relatives one and all is dangerous. They have a passion for sincerity, for immoderate frankness. Noble virtues, no doubt. But who can take it?

And then, if we don't treat them with the due attention they have always merited, on top of

21

everything they go away saying we have no regard for them, that we are conceited, stuck-up, we are high-and-mighty, and we don't want them to come and see us, and all that sort of thing.

My father's right, he lives in the wilds and does without visitors. He lives like a bird, an animal, a creature from space, or something like that. He doesn't like towns and cares nothing for money. A case study. A relic. Guess you could call him a free man, if there is such a thing.

And he will never come. Never ever.

I'm washed up, old 'un.

Help.

The relations are coming, the lot of 'em.

It's a crowd, a multitude, a herd.

An endless procession.

My father won't help me ever again.

And I'm supposed to sleep with all this noise.

At first there were tens, then they became hundreds and went on multiplying by millions.

Impossible to count them.

All I know is that it's the most beautiful procession of little blue coffins, carried by girls and boys dressed in white and blue, in endless uniformed lines. It's just like the National Day. A celebration.

And a great relief: each little coffin is one less mouth in the world.

As a good Christian who does his duty, I follow them.

Sometimes as a bearer, sometimes as an ordinary member of the procession.

From time to time, I strain to discover, somewhere in the blue column, my two little brothers, who cried all night until they breathed their last, like crickets, who sing until they pop.

Wasted effort.

These angels are all alike and the features left their faces long ago.

In the background, the persistently cheerful peal of a bell seems to be telling me, in consolation, that none of them was guilty of being born.

Mocking, indifferent to mournful lamentations, my cousin Calunga beats hell out of a drum and intones a shrill chorus:

> *Onward comrades,*
> *to the flutter of our*
> *pardon*

"It's not pardon, Calunga, it's pennon."

"Just don't put me off. It's got to end in *on*. I want it to rhyme."

> *Onward, without fear,*
> *for in us all*
> *our country trusts*

"That boy's an artist. Takes after his father, good on the saxophone he is."

"As long as he don't end up playing a glass of hooch as good as his father."

> *March we on with gallantry*
> *onwards!*

Now there is a black coffin going past, directly after the blue procession.

And now one bell peals joyfully and another tolls mournfully.

> *Onward, comrades...*

"Slow down Calunga, this sinner's as heavy as lead."

He goes on battering the leather his own way, in his own rhythm, as if he held all the power in the world in his hands.

> *Left, left,*

24

I had a good job on my left.

"Steady on there Calunga. This is a funeral, have you forgotten? You're not at a samba session, nor in the Salvation Army."

Calunga doesn't listen to the bawling out. He doesn't hear the bells. Jubilantly he gets going on another hymn:

> *Glory to the men*
> *the heroes of this land*
> *our beloved homeland*
> *this our Brazil*

Whither goest thou, dainty prince, with sprightly step, marching ever on?

Applause, ladies and gentlemen.

Our applause for these heroic and wonderful children.

Seriously though: who can stand a civic frenzy like this at five in the morning? And on a working day at that. That's to say: without the divine intervention of a national holiday on the calendar.

Let's hope they don't get started on the *God save,* our own popular Sweet oranges / oranges sweet / sweet orange-es / Avocado pear / sweet lime / and tangerine and the Japanese has four children / all of them very sweet and all the rest of a vast repertoire that needs no introduction. If they do I shall throw myself from the window of this fifteenth floor. A case for the police, for the firemen or the first aid? Better: mental home. MADHOUSE. Asylum. Psychiatric clinic (that's

25

more up-to-date). LOONY BIN. Respectable neighbours of the floor above and the next-door apartments, of the floor below, of the entire building, mr. superintendent, sir, dear mr. caretaker, attention mr. doorkeeper, quick mr. cleaner:

Help. SOS. Help. SOS. Help. Urgent, call the men in white.

I've gone round the bend.

"Stop that row."

"Turn that thing down."

"Switch that trash off."

"I'm calling the police."

"I want to sleep."

That's right, they don't make neighbours like they used to.

I want to sleep too, I do.

Though I'm starting to think this is getting amusing.

To tell the truth, there's no electric or electronic gadget switched on here in this pad, no great sound blasting the sound waves, none of those machines that drive people crazy is on and yet the neighbours are all hissing, exploding with anger, shouting from their windows:

"Switch that fucking thing off."

All gone screwy. Fine. Let the sparks fly.

> *Onward comrades,*
> *to the flutter of our*
> *pennon.*

We shall overcome the winter snows,
with faith supreme
in our hearts.

"Provocation. This is provocation."

Right. There is widespread agitation, as it was put in less fortunate times.

"Stop talking, for God's sake. Let me sleep a little longer."

Cristina, my love, I'm sorry if I woke you. (Keep still, don't annoy her. You owe her tonight. Think she noticed what time you came in?)

Just in case, she just gave me a vicious poke with her elbow - what a sharp elbow she has! - followed by a shove. On the follow-through I push my head under the bed to make sure there is no authority, military or civil, tape-recorder in hand, recording the goings-on. Okay, complete paranoia. That *noia* I've carried with me for a long time, if you get my meaning.

Nothing to fear though. For the moment at least, there's no ranking officer, in uniform or civvies, either on or under my bed. They must be asleep in the warmth of the oft-sung splendid cradle, while I can't sleep a wink and my nervous neighbours squirm and demand silence, order and respect. Let them get stuffed. I've never complained about their televisions being too loud, invading my silence late at night. Are you afraid there might be a violent madman here in the block, threatening your peace and your property?

27

Calm yourselves: it's nothing more than a drunkard, but a very well-behaved one. A drunkard who can't make it out of bed to go to the washbasin, stick his finger down his throat and spew everything up. Has any of my neighbours ever had the kindness to visit me, to find out if I'm alive or dead? So, leave me quite alone then, with my little blue coffins. These innocent little souls are incapable of doing harm to anyone. They are just paying me a visit, how shall I put it? - an *evocative* visit, sort of to *remind* me. Well well, to remember is to live, I dreamt of you just yesterday. Miss Teresa's class - that nice kind lady with the pockmarked face who came from somewhere out of town - had been interrupted yet again. And there we went to the church, where we were supposed to make sad faces, stand in file, take hold of the handles and carry the little coffin to the cemetery. But this time (in my dream) the little angel was my cousin Calunga. Halfway to the cemetery he rebelled, causing an almighty uproar. First he opened his eyes, then he sat up in the tiny coffin and began to grow. It was amazing, his transformation from little angel into child and from child into a youth that went on growing and growing. At that stage the procession had stopped, of course.

"Ooooh. It's a miracle," said Miss Teresa. And she fainted.

A flash of lightning lit up the sky, in full daylight. The hot dusty old square, sleepy as ever, suddenly seemed to have gone mad with fear and alarm:

"An angel has come back to life. Come and see with your own eyes."

The children who were holding the handles dumped the coffin on the ground. They could no longer manage Calunga's weight. The others began to chant a welcome to the new-born babe:

>*It's time, it's time.*
>
>*Bum-bum-bum.*
>
>*Ca-lun-ga.*
>
>*Ca-lun-ga.*

As if he meant to prove that he actually was alive, really and truly alive, he picked up the coffin, whose lid he had opened with his own hands when he began to revive. He tipped it over and stepped up onto it, striking a pose like someone mounting a reviewing stand. He said:

"Nobody's going to fucking bury me."

Smiling with excitement, he raised his arm and called for order:

"Attention gang. To the bar. Let's make the most of this break. Let's drinkmemorate."

The people cheered him. The people sang thanksgivings. It was incredible.

"Miracle. Miracle."

"Happiness. No weeping. Let's get smashed," he said.

And the people:

"The little innocent did not go to heaven. He has resuscitated. Praise be to Our Lady of the Sanctuary."

At that point, Big Sarge, our local police chief, as large as life, turned up. A notorious killer of hoodlums. And as always he had his two soldiers with him and a rifle in his hand.

He ordered:

"You're dead, you've got to be buried. Get back in your coffin. Collaborate and avoid a disaster."

The children:

Tag, tag,
hurrah.
It's time, it's time.

"Stop it. That'll do," yelled Big Sarge. "Let's put a stop to this rumpus." And, turning to Calunga: "Come on kid. Into your coffin, smart."

"No son of a bitch is going to bury me in this crappy place," said Calunga. "The place I want to bury myself is between my mother's thighs."

Big Sarge gave the soldiers a signal.

"Fire!"

I woke up.

The shots were from the hill slum, right by my bed.

And now, please leave me in peace with my little blue coffins. Did you hear me, dear neighbours? And don't speak to me of provocation. Kidding maybe, but provocation...

30

By whom?

Could it be some Cuban Connection that slipped into the country via the Guianas, way up there in the Extreme North? Maybe the Russians are coming, with their famous tanks and MIGs? Some Chinese, Cambodian or Vietnamese infiltration, perpetrated from São Paulo's industrial belt? Or merely a ragged-trousered Ethiopian invasion of our national territory via the beaches of the Northeast? Or can it be, no more no less, a direct line from the old, crafty, competent CIA, to destabilize the regime and provoke a new coup d'état? Please to consider the most obvious: a grave-diggers' revolt. They must be pissed off having to bury so many kids. But let's get to the point: what is actually inside these simple coffins? Innocent little children or heavy armaments?

Onward, comrades...

And attention, pay attention. The noise you can hear now is the noise of tin cans. That's what I said: TI-IN CANS.

And this really is provocation. And it is a routine scene at the foot of the hill, at my very bedside. The target: the stubborn inhabitant of a shack squeezed between two high-rises, like an ant flattened by the feet of two elephants, and facing a huge derelict building, which stretches from end to end of the block and for that reason got the name Maracanã. (Attention, folks: we not only have the biggest stadium in the world. We now have the biggest apartment block on the planet. Pack your things and hot-foot it to Rio. There's always room for one more.)

The cans come from the windows opposite. The offender bitches. And the more he appeals, the more cans rain down on his roof. Champion of cleanliness, of politeness and good habits, this solitary boxer got himself a fight in which he is losing every round. Even so he doesn't give up. He keeps getting more and more angry, insolent and cocky. It's a daily war of cans against words. The words being rebukes, notions of hygiene, lessons in morality and public-spiritedness. After all, he is the grandson of a field-marshal - do you know who you are playing with? Every blessed day he warns: there is a barrel of gunpowder in his backyard. One of these days he'll send everything up in flames. But for the time being, despite his threats, he has only tried to make the shower opposite understand that it is much more decent to deposit their garbage in the dump than to throw it through the windows.

"Scum. Slum-trash. Pigs."

Answer: cans.

"Bums. Why don't you go back to the pigsties you should never have left?"

Answer:

"Shut your mouth, loony."

Counter-attack:

"Cowards. Come out from behind your shutters.

32

Show your faces."

Answer:

Cans, sticks, stones, bottles. Assorted torpedoes.

They've made a clown of the field-marshal's grandson. Or a plaything.

One of these days I shall go down there just to tell him this:

"They're having fun at your expense, friend. You're playing the fool's part."

During a respite, of course. I don't want to catch the shrapnel.

Onward comrades...

In the intervals between bombardments he plays the banjo. When he gets tired of his favourite instrument he puts on a record. Nearly always of old nostalgic blues. A touch of serenity in our frenzied blitzkrieg, in which the tempo of the hours is thumped out in powerful decibels, bursts of gunfire, shouts for help and shouts of stop thief, so that no one pays attention any more. Being a field-marshal's grandson is as much of an anachronism as playing the banjo, listening to blues and living in a shack that's not even coveted by the building industry.

Console yourself friend. I'm way up here, scraping the sky, but with two windows busted by a couple of mortar volleys. Courtesy of one of those opposite, during the last World Cup. "Recuerdos" of two blinding goals by Brazil. I didn't get to see the marksman's face, that valiant national champion of window shooting. At the time I was watching the match on television. When I heard the explosions, I rushed into the sitting-room just to check the damage: bits of glass, the smell of gunpowder and the threat of fire. I decided never to replace the glass. There will be more World Cups.

No one here will stop us...

"Stop talking, damn you."

My wife reckons I'm always talking to myself now. I talk to myself in my sleep, I talk to myself when I wake up, I talk to myself while I shower, I talk to myself when I shave. She reckons I'm going mad.

Well, I still haven't said the main thing. In plain words, I'm still drunk.

And it's five in the morning already. Or rather: it's still five in the morning.

Last night I was shepherded off to a grand party at a consul's house, by a character I hadn't seen for years and years, and first we went to have one to celebrate our reunion and then he said come with me, you'll enjoy it and we can carry on talking, hell, it's been so long since we saw one another, and there's me thinking shall I go or shan't I, my idea was just a quick one, while the traffic was thinning out, going back home straight after finishing work with all those giant traffic jams was a pain, better to give it a while, a short while, but a junket was not on the books, I need to get to work early tomorrow, I've got a meeting at nine

34

sharp, I shan't stay long either, he said, let's go, there'll be a bunch of beautiful people, it'll be fun, knows his way around he does, I thought, name must be on everybody's tongue, I need to phone home, I said, and he said how's...? Cristina's fine, I said, Cris, of course, Cris, he said, one never knows if one's friends are still with the same one, hence my hesitation, I have to let her know, in fact I'm going to ask her if she wants to come along, send her a kiss from me, he said, so you're still together? She doesn't want to go out tonight, says she's very tired, I said, coming back from the telephone, sounds impossible, he said, people our age are into their fifth marriage, I've gone through three myself, she sends you a kiss, thanks, so Cris still remembers me? Said he, and me thinking why is this character so insistent on my company? Must be badly in need of somebody to talk to, whether it's me or someone else, but isn't he a guest at the party, won't he meet a "bunch of beautiful people"? And I found myself thinking again that I only wanted a quiet drink to let the traffic thin out and to put my thoughts in order, you die a little every day, at the end of the day's work, you urgently need a drink to feel that you're alive, you need to feel that in your very skin, in the thrill you feel with the first glassful, an injection throbbing in your blood, deadening and exhilarating at the same time, get drunk, so said the poet Charles Baudelaire "on wine, poetry or virtue", but with a fucking heat like this, wine's not on, it's either iced beer or *caipirinha*, or a whisky on the rocks, if your pocket stretches to it, but poetry and virtue will never cure anybody's hangover, so let's drink to the postponement of the agony of tomorrow's obligations or to a slow death, which comes to the same thing, there'll be women galore there, he said, but what I was thinking about was my work, about something I'd heard in the corridor at the agency about staff changes, seems the management isn't too pleased with the team's performance, they're talking of the need for new blood, people with more dash, more brilliance, zip, spunk, in a word: people with more AMBITION, I'm progressing step-by-dangerous-step into my forties, I've already lost the will to win, how long before I walk the plank? Today is a perfect day to go to a party, of course, why didn't I think of it before? a party! splendid idea, one invitee invites a hundred, etc., my friend talked and talked and talked and I thought today's the day Cris is going to kick my ass, today she's going to turn me out, because today I'm going to get screwed, well haven't I met an old chum? he talks like crap, unbosoms himself so easily I'd be embarrassed if I were paying the slightest attention, the guy seems to have been doing well in business, but his private life looks to be rather complicated, with all sorts of fights with his ex-wives, problems of alimony and legal threats - "not paying child support is the only thing that means jail in this country, did you know that?" - and we arrived at the consul's house, where I became quite convinced that the evening was promising. Truly! Astral high in High Leblon.

Outcome: I got back at cock-crow after losing sight of my "friend". Worse: I didn't make it with anyone and now I'm suffering from a dreadful hangover, talking to the bedroom walls and counting little blue coffins. Long time no see, eh, my little angels? (That was how it all started). Long time no see, eh? What y'been doing, what're y'doing, hell, let's catch up on the news. This and that, on to a bar. Lift (I had no car), party. Take the beach road always the nicest. All roads lead to High Leblon. It's lighter along the Avenida Atlantica. It's plenty light in the Vieira Souto. The Delfim Moreira is dazzling. *This is a beautiful Rio: sun, sex and sea.* And a night full of stars. My "friend" was telling me he was on his own, "free, free, absolutely free" and that he never missed a party now. And the more he talked, the more I was struck by a silly memory: a sentence read many moons ago in a book by a legendary drunkard, the late Scott Fitzgerald, who wrote about "this highfalutin city talk". No. I wasn't remembering my father yet, the pile of beans, the divine sleep I had lying on it, nor the kids who didn't have any beans, the ones in the little blue coffins on their way to heaven, and I didn't want to hear a lullaby yet, nor was I thinking about my cousin Calunga, my best bar-crawling crony, not these air-conditioned executive bars after office hours, but the low popular dives when we were adults, in the

37

early hours, in Salvador, the capital of the state where we were born, and in São Paulo and Rio de Janeiro, not counting the years of our *apprenticeship* in a town in the interior, when we mixed vermouth or rum with our coffee, in a cup, so no one would suspect, with the connivance of the bar owners, who, with a completely straight face, broke the law forbidding the sale of alcoholic drinks to under-eighteens.

This wasn't at all what I was thinking about when I went over to that panoramic window, that "wide-screen view", on one of the topmost floors of one of the latest monuments to the Construction Industry erected in High Leblon. And I confess, though I was not in the least concerned with the "drama" of the consul, who my "friend Free" had said was "in need of a boost", poor guy, he's leaving, been transferred to Tegucigalpa, just think, he of all people, who loves Brazil, a-DORES Rio, which made my head take a turn round the map of the Americas to locate Tegucigalpa, until I remembered that Honduras had sent a bunch of rookies, whose innocence won them my approval and good will, to the world war that was waged on Spanish swards in 1982, as I was saying, though indifferent to the existential problems of diplomatic life, I couldn't help wondering if that consul would ever get a second opportunity to own a window like that. "Life is much more successfully looked at from a single window." Scott Fitzgerald rapped on my forehead again. Yes, it was he I was thinking about. And the resurrection of my twenties. Fitzgerald in my mind went with the party and, for a perfectly explicable reason, he also went with São Paulo, much more than with Rio de Janeiro, for the simple reason that it was in São Paulo that I discovered him, when I was working in an office situated next door to a mansion in the elegant Pacaembu suburb. At lunchtime, while I munched a sandwich, I immersed myself in the pages of his book, reading on into office hours and, when I left the office in the late afternoon, I always had a last look at the mansion next door, absolutely dying to knock on the door and ask if the Great Gatsby lived there. "He had come a long way, to this blue lawn, and his dream must have seemed so close that he could hardly fail to grasp it. He did not know that it was already behind him, somewhere back in that vast obscurity beyond the city, where the dark fields of the republic rolled on under the night."

The consul didn't have a blue lawn. But in exchange he had a whole shining city at his feet. Standing by his "cinemascope" window, he could easily lose his breath several times a day in order to have the pleasure of recovering it with the certainty that all that really did exist, yes, it was true: *sun, sex and sea* - and millions of stars. The Great Gatsby had never known anything like that. Nor did São Paulo. My head went whirling again around the map of the Americas: could there be a High Leblon in Tegucigalpa?

"Gatsby believed in the green light, the orgiastic future that year by year recedes before us. It eluded us then, but that's no matter - tomorrow we will run faster, stretch out our arms farther... And one fine morning -

"So we beat on, boats against the current, borne back ceaselessly into the past."

It must have been because I was so driven on by my book and by my curiosity to know if the Great Gatsby lived next door, that at the end of the month I was thrown out of my job. The excuse was a cut in the budget, but secretly I knew that the real reason was my lack of productivity. São Paulo did not invite me to its parties in any mansion in Pacaembu and furthermore gave me its first lesson: reading during office time got you your cards.

My wife (Dona Cris) gives me another violent poke with her elbow.

"You wrestled all the time in bed and you still wake up moaning. Do me a favour, next time you come home drunk sleep somewhere else. I can't stand this un-bear-able stench making the whole room smell foul."

One eye on the alarm clock and the other wanting to go on sleeping. And the little blue coffins. And the shooting up in the *favela*. It's always like this. When it isn't samba, what is it? Bullets. *Our* favela's carnival club gave it all they'd got all through the year, working late into the night at rehearsals, which always ended in fireworks. (Try and sleep with a samba like that.) But they got their reward: they pocketed the championship award in the Avenida Rio Branco. I was pleased with the news, which I read in the papers. The prize-winning squad up there is now rocking to the sound of bullets. Don't get over-heated, guys. Let's warm up the drums. More to come next carnival.

Why did I have so much to drink at the consul's house?

Five o'clock in the morning. A hot stuffy morning, the exact temperature of my hangover. I may not know what day it is or what month we're in, but I sure can't forget that it's summer. Five o'clock in the morning, summer time. Four o'clock on the old scale. Maybe the clock has stopped. Will it always be five o'clock in the morning, summer time, for the rest of my life?

I tried a few steps at the consul's house and felt ridiculous. Someone jolted my arm and the contents of my glass spilled onto an immaculate white dress. I felt obnoxious. I slipped away to one of the rooms, where a small group intimated I should be quiet: the consul was reading poetry. Or rather: they were all watching the consul reading poetry on the television. It was a cassette tape (a video!) he had recorded of himself. "A great artist," someone said, only to be hushed by another request for silence. At that point one of the ladies nudged her neighbour to attract her atttention to the gesture she was making with her closed hand,

moving it up and down at the level of her erogen-
ous zone. I understood. It was a merciless criticism
of the consul's poetry.

"Well-bred young ladies also know how you
beat your meat," I thought and escaped into
another room, where I slumped down and found
myself in a library. It was there that I came face to
face with Ernesto Che Guevara. I got a fright.
"What are you doing here?" Che didn't so much
as blink. Speechless he was, speechless he
remained. Who would guess, eh, Comandante?
Decorating a diplomat's bookshelves, eh? Che was
not even there, this chitchat didn't concern him. At
that moment I remembered my cousin Calunga: he
had a portrait of Che Guevara too, carved in
wood, adorning one wall of a one-room apartment
in Copacabana. And I thought of calling the consul
and telling him that this sort of decorative article
was outmoded in my country. But I controlled
myself: I'd already disgraced myself once and it
would hardly be diplomatic to repeat the achieve-
ment. I took another long, close look at Che's face.
"Who brought you here, eh? Are you a guest of a
guest, like me? But of course, you were brought by
the owner himself, who, finding you abandoned,
solito, in the bowels of some old curiosity shop, felt
the hell sorry for you and decided to ensconce you
in the comfort of a library. An excellent place for
you, isn't it? Along with the books. I had a cousin,
you know, his name was Calunga. He worked in a
newspaper and later in television. He died of

drink. But he was not frivolous like the crowd that's here. And he was a fan of yours. Big fan. Real fan. So much so that his first child was called Ernesto, in your honour, of course. You were the only idol he ever had, in his whole life. My cousin Calunga actually had your photograph on his wall, right bang in the beginning of the seventies, when your picture meant jail and even certain death. But you know what Calunga would say if he knew you'd ended up in this library? "Fucking hell, even Che's turned into a mosquito on an upper-crust bum." A disillusioned member of your old fan club, you understand. Sorry and all that. Hasta luego. Hasta siempre.

And I began to sidle out slowly, trying to keep my balance, one foot after the other. I didn't aim to make another blunder. Then I saw a famous actress wiggling her hips in the lounge. I tried to dance with her, but I heard some mocking laughs. Ballsed it up again, goddam stupid. My glass fell and smashed on the floor. There was applause. The consul gave me another glass, which he made a point of filling himself. Genuine Scotch, and plenty of it. There'll be no shortage of that in Tegucigalpa, that's for sure. When I made my first attempt to leave, I realized that the door was locked and someone had hidden the key. The consul recited another of his poems, live this time, and everyone clapped. He recited them in his own language, Spanish. In fact, the vast majority of those present were speaking only Spanish, even

43

the Brazilian guests. I was undoubtedly a foreigner there. What a night! A typical etylico-literary soiree by the pool, in sight of the XXIst century. The world going up in flames and there we were singing, dancing, getting plastered and disgracing ourselves. The consul was bellowing his country's heartburn at the top of his voice, all those songs that Usted jamás olvidará, oh my adolescence soaked in Merino rum, patchouli - the cheapest perfume - clap and gonorrhoea, in the brothels of a far-off Brazil, when life was a dream and not this wretched hangover. A splendid night. If you can get yourself an invite, Rio will always be a party.

I must sleep, sleep, sleep, sleep. Another sixty minutes, thirty minutes, ten minutes, a few seconds. In a little while I have to get on stage, all spry and cheerful, ready to perform for a whole day.

Give me strength.

Forty years old.

When I was twenty, they stuffed a dictatorship down my throat.

Now I've reached maturity I have to carry the weight of my exhaustion. Where's the fun in that?

My cousin went at forty. Must've been able to foresee what was coming.

You see, Calunga, you missed the brilliant conclusion one of our crowd came to, just before he gulped down one for the road and left the drinking dive for good:

"Until I was twenty I believed in Holy Mother Church. Between twenty and thirty, I believed in the Communist Party. From thirty to forty, I believed in Psychoanalysis. Now all I believe in is a full line on a bingo card."

And he went off to do battle.

Attention now, your full attention. New images on the wall: tanks. Battle tanks on top of the blue coffins.

São Paulo, 31st March 1964.

4 in the afternoon.

Urgent.

"It's on the radio," said a distressed mother on the telephone. That was it: Mackenzie University was up in arms. And her daughter was in there.

São Paulo, 31st March 1964.

4.30 in the afternoon.

Urgent.

I am stopped at the entrance to Mackenzie.

Students go in and out. Out and in.

I ask after a girl called Luciana.

Nobody has time to answer.

I go over to the other side of the street, corner of Maria Antonia.

The tanks start arriving.

They advance slowly, their huge caterpillars rolling over the asphalt.

Retractable guns sliding out of their gun turrets and rotating, round and round.

Machine guns appear at the windows and take aim.

São Paulo, 31st March 1964.

5 in the afternoon.

Urgent.

Mackenzie students applaud the arrival of the tanks.

A shower of confetti floods the street, at the entrance to Mackenzie.

It's a ball.

São Paulo, 31st March. Night.

Everybody looking for everybody else. Everybody running away from everybody. The news is contradictory. There is talk of many arrests.

I find my cousin Calunga in the usual bar. He was already drunk. As usual.

"C'n only happen in Brazil," another drunk shouts. "A revolution without shedding a drop of blood, only in Brazil. Three cheers for Brazil!"

"What fucking revolution!" said Calunga. "A barracks putsch like in any banana republic. And the people are unarmed."

"But who'll swear that there won't be plenty of blood spilt?" I ask. "There are troops advancing from Minas Gerais to Rio, there's hope the Northeast will resist and in the south..."

"I'm talking of our temperament," the other drunk philosophized. "Pacific. That's it. We're a peaceful people. That adores a bit of fun and games, a samba, a game of football. And fuck the world. Fuck revolutions."

Calunga got steamed up:

"That's stupid. A bunch of half-starved cretins, with no blood in our veins, destroyed by inanition and ignorance, and you come with this temperament nonsense. Fuck your temperament!"

"Take it easy," I said. "The putsch was in Brasilia. We're in São Paulo."

"And in a bar," said Calunga. "Know what? Tomorrow I shan't go to the newspaper, I'm not going to work. It'll be a long time before I set foot in that fucking place again. I'm in mourning. I've gone on strike. I'm going to get stewed twenty-four hours a day the next few days, or the next few years. Waiter, bring another one! And the next one to say anything about the Brazilian people's good nature gets a wallop."

Good times. We didn't yet know what was coming.

"You can bring another," said Calunga.

That night I dreamed about my mother.

She was dressed as if she'd just come from mass.

She had her head covered with a black shawl which fell over her shoulders.

She had a rosary in one hand and a prayerbook in the other.

I thought: that was just the way I saw her on the day of her last communion. She hasn't changed a bit.

And Momma had that huge belly again, like she had every year. She was expecting again, she was still pregnant, like she always was.

And she was praying. For God to forgive her her sins and give her peace everlasting - the everlasting Amen. For Him to bless her children. For Our Lady of Easy Births to give her an easy time. For God to send rain every winter - for the bounty, abundance and prosperity of our desert lands.

"And deliver us, Lord, from atheists and communists."

Momma died in that childbirth. She left a load of children. That time Our Lady of Easy Births did not give her an easy time.

"Your blessing, Momma."

"Ah, I'm so pleased to find you. God alone knows how I've worried."

"I thought only the living worried."

"The news, son. This confusion. I was fit to tear my hair out."

I thought: she still can't manage to rest in peace.

"Don't worry, Momma. Things are under control."

"Well I was dead scared it was a civil war."

"You can relax. It's not a civil war, not yet."

"Thanks be to God," she said. "Now, tell me something: aren't you afraid of living so high up? Goodness me, what a crazy height. Don't you get dizzy?"

"Yes, it really is high up. Twenty-three floors. But you get used to it."

"And this room. What a mess. It's filthy, And what a funny smell. And not even a saint on the wall. Not a single image of Our Lady!"

I almost tell her: it's because Calunga is always drunk and sometimes he spills drink on the floor and occasionally he misses his aim in the john. But I didn't think it right to put the blame on the friend who was sharing expenses with me in that tiny apartment - my cousin Calunga, her nephew.

"When I wake up I'll tidy up. You're right. It's an awful mess."

"You haven't noticed anything?"

"I only noticed that you are here, paying me a visit."

"Is that all?"

I pretended I was thinking, as if I was trying to guess something.

"You don't mean to tell me you haven't noticed the toy I brought you," she sighed. She seemed a bit keyed-up.

"A toy? Come on Mother, I'm not a kid any more."

49

"But this toy is different. You'll like it. Now look. Take a good look. It's right here in front of you. You can't possibly fail to see it."

I got a fright. It really was a very strange present. Huge. And all lights. At first I thought it must be a flying saucer, just like the ones you see in magazine photos.

"What the devil's this?"

"A battle tank," she said. "But this is quite different from any you've ever seen. It can come in and out of your room without breaking the windows."

"But how?"

"This is a magic tank. Like it?"

"Of course, Mother. You're not real."

"Now let me go."

"No, no. Wait a bit. Let me go to the kitchen and find something for us to nibble. Aren't you hungry?"

"It's ages since I knew what it's like to be hungry. I must be going, before it starts to grow light. The dead only have permission to go around by night, you know."

And she disappeared.

What a pity. I swear I was itching to know what it was like in eternity, whether God and the devil exist, if heaven, hell and purgatory really exist and in which of them she had found shelter. I also wanted to know if by any chance she knew if I was going to live long and be happy, and which place was reserved for me after death.

And since I had lost the opportunity of finding answers for such transcendental questions, I decided to go out into the night and enjoy myself a bit. São Paulo also had its charms; well, didn't it? Good food and drink, etc. Night dives for all pockets and brothels for all classes. "Buy me a drink, honey?"

But first I needed to show off my Magic Object to someone - a very special "someone", who would admire me, pamper me, swoon at my feet, begging for a ride in my new, extraordinary, fantastic, fabulous chariot. A magic battle tank! I had to fly in search of Luciana, the girl who occasionally went to the cinema with me and who, when we came out, would "explain" the message of the film we'd just seen, but who was not always available to keep me company, a drink afterwards, a kiss, a bit of petting, at times she would appear with the most inviting smile in the world and disappear again, swallowed up in student life, meetings, committees, parties - leaving me nursing my pride, crazy with jealousy.

"To Mackenzie," I ordered. And whoosh! Off I went, flying my battle tank high above the lights of São Paulo. Magic!

A kid raced desperately towards the exit, pursued by troops with batons, police dogs and an athletic bunch of well-nourished students who looked as if they were running a marathon against the dogs and the men in uniform.

"Luciana! Run!"

I thought her eyes would pop out of her head, when they caught sight of the tank at the entrance to Mackenzie. She looked behind her and her pursuers were very close. She felt cornered. I realized she was turning to one side in order to scale a wall. I shouted:

"No! You'll hurt yourself. Come here. Run. This is a pretend tank. I've come to fetch you."

She came and I grabbed her by the hair and pulled her into my Magic Object.

"To Pacaembu," I ordered. And whoosh! We took off. The troops down below started firing. But my "Magic" flew faster than their bullets.

"Steady. Hang on there. Hold tight."

She took a small mirror from her purse. She looked at herself.

"I'm an awful mess," she said.

"Not at all. You look more like a national heroine. Glory at last."

"Oh, get lost."

She found a comb and tidied her hair. Then she put some lipstick on.

"Where are we heading for?" she said.

"To Pacaembu."

"No! Football? Now?"

"I said to Pacaembu. Not to the Pacaembu stadium. We're going to a party."

52

"Party? Are you crazy? What I want is water. Quick, or I'll die."

"There'll be plenty of water at the party. From tapple to tipple. Don't worry. But first I have to do a little job, at a neighbouring house. Easy, easy. There'll be water. I know exactly where the fridge is. And please to give me a kiss."

"Mmm."

"That was really good."

"You deserve it."

I ordered:

"Shatter everything."

Crash! The humble office where I failed to make the grade as a junior writer of press releases crumbled like a matchbox under an elephant's foot. Luciana, with a bottle in her hand, was gulping down water and sobbing with laughter.

"I never saw such a crazy thing," she said. "It's marvellous."

"Right. Those bastards'll never fire anybody again. Not here, at any rate."

Luciana applauded:

"Bravo! Beautiful!"

Then she kissed me again, without my having to ask. And it was some kiss. Tongue in mouth. Tongue with tongue. We were eating each other. I put my hand between her thighs, slowly, caressing her, rubbing her there, tout est là. Luciana knew French, qu'est-ce que l'amour? She was a high-class girl and she was all wet. Marvellous.

"Now let's go to the Great Gatsby's house."

"What?"

"To the party! Have you forgotten?"

"But the Great Gatsby is only a character. A book...that you lent me."

"Have you read it yet?"

"Yes."

"Did you like it?"

"Not much."

"Why?"

"I prefer the..."

"Proletarian novel?"

"Yes."

"I thought as much. All the more reason for you to meet the Great Gatsby. *In person.*"

"But he doesn't exist. He's only..."

"He does exist. He lives next door and he's giving a party in honour of the men who set the dogs on you. A party for God, Family and Country. Look how brightly lit-up it is. And look at all those big cars, all those Mercedes Benz, all those armed soldiers guarding the entrance. God bless us!"

"Are you crazy enough to want to go there? They'll kill us. Their tanks are for real."

"That's what I mean to see," I said resolutely.

And I gave the command:

"Enter."

"Oooh," they all went, when we parked in the

garden. It wasn't a blue lawn, like in Scott Fitz-gerald's book. It was more like a rainbow.

"Password, please," said a somewhat befuddled voice trying to sound firm, through a walkie-talkie.

"Gatsby."

"Who?"

"Gatsby. The Great Gatsby."

"It's the American force. They did come. They've arrived late, but they are here."

Popping of flashbulbs and clink of glasses. "Chin-chin." "Make yourselves at home. *Welcome.* Everything's under control already."

"Thanks a lot," I said. *"We love Brazil."*

They took photos of my Magic Tank, asked what year it was - "latest model, very latest model" - and if I had any idea how much it cost in dollars and if it could be imported already. Naturally, but naturally, there was no small amount of lavish praise for North America's *unbeatable* technology. (Here, now and for the future.)

"To tell the truth, I was given it. It was a pre-sent from my mother. *My poor and very nice Mother."*

"Oooh," and they all laughed and said I was also very nice and very funny. *Funny guy.* ·

And so it went. All very pleasant, nice, "amus-ing". A "muy hermoso" world, as Calunga would say indignantly, referring to the banana republics.

"Oh darling, I can't possibly start the new *saison*

55

without one of those," said a jovial lady three elbows away.

"You must be joking," said the gentleman I assumed to be her husband. His tone of voice was unquestionably polite.

"Not at all," replied the melodious female voice with a ripple of her body that really locked my attention onto the tinkle of her charm: "This tank is going to be a great success, it will dictate fashion. Le dernier cri. Those who don't have one won't have a thing."

"She's right," intervened another elegant gentleman. "In fact, I think the matter should be on the agenda for our next meeting, which, in any case, will be tomorrow. This tank will be the greatest symbol of modern Brazil. We have to think what the country can gain with it, not only in internal terms, but also on the external market. Indeed, I want to launch right here the slogan which shall be the platform for the country to get out of the Stone Age: *Exportation is the solution.* We must address to the War Ministry our first great revolutionary proposal: a tank factory. The Finance Ministry will have to agree. Let us go right to the top. It's a different story now."

"A factory to make tanks like this one?" asked the lady who was crazy to have the same model as my divine Magic Object.

"Exactly," said the one I supposed was the author-to-be of the tank factory proposal. "Exactly the same. It's a beautiful tank."

"What an automobile!" sighed the lovely lady. "What a chariot!"

"Alright, alright," said her husband. "Tomorrow we'll put the matter on the agenda."

"But what I think, darling," the lovely lady snuggled up to his shoulder, "is that this factory idea is a medium- or long-term project. I so wanted a present like this now... Oh, darling, you do understand, don't you?" And lowering her voice, and with a discreet glance around her: "I did so want to be the first, don't you see?"

"Alright, alright," he said.

"You really are a darling," she said.

Three cheers for Momma, I thought. The magic tank she gave me was breaking some hearts.

"When I was a kid, the only tank I knew was the one Momma fetched the water in for us to drink and wash ourselves. It was also where she used to wash our clothes. But, despite her struggles, she never stopped believing in the American dream. I think it was worth it. I am very moved by this great welcome you are giving me, all of you. But for the present Momma gave me, I could never have been here today, joining in this party. 31st of March! I shall never forget this date."

"A party for the people of Brazil," said the enthusiastic lady.

"Thanks a lot for everything," I said. "*I love Brazil.*"

"And São Paulo? What do you think of São Paulo?" asked the same polite, elegant lady.

"I love São Paulo too. It reminds me of Chicago, the city where I was born."

"You are very nice. *But I love Paris.* Toujours Paris."

"You have excellent taste," I said, as I was dragged away by my beloved Luciana. Jealousy? And I was really doing quite well, wasn't I?

"My God," Luciana whispered in my ear. "What a cool performer you are. I just love it."

"Keep cool. We'll eat and have a spree and afterwards..."

"What, afterwards?"

"You'll see."

We were eating and drinking, all the very best, when the annoying part of the program began. The requests, the commissions.

Could we take a little present for the President of the United States? Oh, yes, of course. It will be an honour. But I froze when I saw the size and the value of the thing: a tree all in fine wood, covered in mother-of-pearl, six feet tall and weighing nearly 300 pounds. And more: a huge eagle made of the same materials. For the First Lady, the souvenirs were no less lavish: luxurious ball gowns covered in sequins, satin-lined boxes and a gilt vibrator chair for massages. And on top of that, a ton of minor trinkets: gold Cartier watches, with the effigy of a general, a six-foot Christmas tree adorned with white shells and a huge pineapple coated with emeralds.

"This is for you," and they placed a gold Cartier on my wrist. It was beautiful, no doubt. But the annoying thing was to have to look at a general's face every time I wanted to see the time.

"Is this so's I won't arrive late next time?"

Laughter. *You're a funny guy. Really.* A great guy.

I thought: this will all go to the drought victims and the flood victims, etc. The majority are right here in São Paulo. And when I whispered my plan to Luciana, she muttered that the poor needed neither presents nor charity, and I hissed:

"Clam up, this is no time for speeches and sermons."

And she:

"You're just a crazy, alienated petty-bourgeois."

"Is that so? Then you can start by giving me that pretty diamond necklace you have round your neck. And go back to your place in the Magic Tank, because you are now about to see the best part. We're getting out of here."

She got it immediately. And said, with a spark of mischief at the corner of her mouth, on the tip of her nose, in the speck in her eye:

"Give 'em the works, kiddo."

Clever girl, Luciana. Okay, Baby. *Go home.*

Then I ordered my great tank, Momma's lovely

marvellous present:

"Wipe it out."

The alarm went off, next to my bed, like a bomb. Why now? Fuck it.

"How about a hair of the dog?"

"You're crazy. I'm going to work."

"Well I'm in mourning. I went on strike, remember? I am going to get stewed."

(One moment, please, Dona Cris here is wanting a word. Is she going to remind me once more that at that time - the day when Momma gave me a magic tank - she was just a kid playing with dolls? Let's hear what she has to say. Your turn, my dear):

"Drinking is undignified."

"Drunkards are all pitiable."

"Nobody loves a drunkard."

And me:

"Only drunkards see the world go round."

And mine is going round. Like a wallflower.

Wake up, Cris. Wake up and pray. There goes the procession passing by, winding past like a snake just sliding by.

This cortege was scheduled for later, when the sun was on its downward curve towards the west. Who can stand being stuck underneath this god-awful fireball, and with a heavy cross on their shoulder into the bargain? I guess we shall have processions all day today, from sun-up to sundown. Should be a good show. Keep watching, Cris dear.

There will be people with their feet bleeding from the thorns, knees getting torn on the rocks, and a caterwauling chorus appealing to heaven for the rain that just won't come. The high point will be when the men sink a cross on the very top of a hill called Mercy. Wait and you shall see.

Look now, esteemed viewer, at the first one to come on the scene, just as day is breaking.

Do not imagine him to be a penitent the same as the others. He is a very special sinner. A real artist.

Every morning, at daybreak, he arrives and installs himself here on this corner, where he stays, silent and impassive, moving only in accordance with the position of the sun. All means have been tried, some of them not very commendable, to make him speak, but in vain. Some people even throw stones at him or toss him peanuts. Reprehensible mischief, of course. As well as being quiet and inoffensive, he is the only tourist attraction in a place that is poor in economic resources and frequently scourged both by drought and by great floods.

But who, then, is this man?

That, ladies and gentlemen, is exactly the question our program will attempt to answer. After the break.

No one knows his name, his origin, his story.

With the passing of time, however, he has earned a certain public respect, which may also be interpreted as the acquisition of a right: the right to be where and how he wants. The right to have his place in the world, where he is a nuisance to nobody.

His behaviour is exemplary according to the spontaneous declarations of all our interviewees in the environs. We are therefore in the presence of a new phenomenon, a challenge to man's imagination: standing all day on a street corner, moving only, as we already said, in accordance with the sun's motion, it is believed that this man is a new time machine, someone who changed himself by magic into time itself. There are, however, those who claim that he is a daytime ghost. This is fantastic. And it is the subject we are going to discuss. Phenomenon or phantom? Let us now go over to our experts, all well-known specialists whose seriousness is unquestioned. In just one minute, please. After the commercials.

"Stop bugging me, damn you. Can't you see I'm only a sunflower?"

(My eye, the one that's fixed on the wall, opens wide. I've cracked the charade. Calunga. The scoffer. Come over here, cousin. Let's have a jaw.)

And he:

"Will you kindly explain to me what this rumpus is about?"

"The TV gang, the journalists, your old colleagues. Have you forgotten already what it was like?"

"And those others, so how shall I put it, fossilized?"

"All high class people. Scholars, professors, real heavyweights."

"Shall we have one?"

"Steady on, pal. It's early still and I've got a stinking hangover."

"There's no way I'm going along with this business dry."

"Do your best to keep calm. They might call the men in white."

"But who are they?"

"The ones who explain everything. Exegetes, hermeneuticists, researchers, educationalists and phenomenologists. This last lot have come from Brasilia. They specialize in the paranormal."

"You don't say? Lord save us."

"Come to us," said one of those from Brasilia. "We have the key to the gate of the Third Millennium."

"I thought that Brasilia crowd had the key to prison."

"That was in the past. Brasilia is now the key of hope."

"Is that still the last thing to die?" asked Calunga.

"He does speak. That is the main thing and we had not yet noticed. He speaks," the exegete was jumping up and down in his chair.

One of the researchers starts getting impatient. He clears his throat. He drinks a glass of water. He has a notebook in front of him. It looks as if he simply can't wait to have his say. His text is all ready and he is taking not the slightest notice of what is going on. But someone else gets in first:

"I am a poet and I realize that what is happening here is one of the most exciting moments Brazilian television has ever been able to show. In honour of this splendid moment we are living through, I am going to read a poem."

And he read:

> *Ah, Sunflower! weary of time,*
> *Who countest the steps of the sun,*
> *Seeking after that sweet golden clime*
> *Where the traveller's journey is done.*

Everyone applauded. Except, of course, the researcher, who opened his notebook and went ahead:

"Before I start, there are two things I want to say."

"Be ye Mexican?" asked Calunga. "I've heard that beginning once before, at the cinema. In Cantinflas's time, remember him?"

Laughter. The presenter asks for quiet.

The researcher didn't let Calunga's mockery get

him down. He went on:

"To simplify matters and go straight to the point: I would like to hear your impressions of your extraordinary experience as a triple being: dead-resurrected-enchanted."

"All a sunflower knows is how to turn in the same direction as the sun," said Calunga, with a mischievous snicker.

More laughter. The presenter endeavours to bring the panel to order.

"Well I think," said the exegete, "that what matters is what your are: a phenomenon."

"Well I never. I didn't know about that," said Calunga.

"As far as I am concerned," the exegete went on, "the whole of human knowledge is not enough to explain you. It matters little to me whether at some time in your life an alarm clock chased you tick-tock tick-tock until it blew your head off. Nor is there any point in advancing theories about its being the blare of rock-and-roll, an inadequate diet, excess of alcohol, drug abuse, the epistemological divide, the effects of the atom bomb, economic instability, disappointment in love, loss of identity, late arrival at work due to the bad quality of the transport system, food poisoning caused by agricultural effluent, noise and atmospheric pollution, lack of ego gratification despite life's rewards, syphilis, x-ray and laser beam. What matters to me, what is really interesting, is that you are an example. An irrefutable example of enchantment. A living example that as a people we are, first and foremost, magical."

"It was all because of my mother's thighs," said Calunga.

Laughter. Turmoil. Clash of opinions among the members of the panel.

End of discussion.

Commercials.

Magnificent Calunga. You were great.

Hey, hey, where've you gone?

He's gone off into a different orbit. He's skipped it.

He comes and goes. Before long he'll be back again, leading the chorus in the blue procession:

Onward comrades...

Give it to 'em, kiddo.

"Between a woman and a bottle, a drunkard prefers the bottle."

Ah, dearest Cris, don't exaggerate. I love you, believe me I do.

Wake up and come and see what I can see. Incredible things are happening on our wall.

But I insist: I must sleep. SLEEP. A few more minutes, a few seconds, an hour, half an hour, two hours. Until my time is come, the sound of the gong, the factory hooter, the whistle for my own penalty. I woke up two hours too early, that's what happened. And I stayed that way: one eye trying to sleep, the other on the alarm clock. And the little blue coffins and the black coffin and the armoured tanks and my cousin Calunga's piercing voice and all the rest.

Calunga: ex-student of the country school in the ex-district of Back of Beyond, Bahia.

Ex-marksman at training school number something or other in a jumped-up town in the same State.

Ex-reporter of the waterfront, the morgue and of many late night police shifts in the capital.

Ex-war hero in peacetime, thanks to a courageous mission undertaken by the Glorious Brazilian Army, initially viewed as a glorious piece of idiocy, but subsequently inscribed in the annals of our history: the Bahia-to-Brasilia march, on foot, the arrival of which was timed to coincide with the inauguration of Brazil's new capital city.

For the record, everything turned out right. In addition, without injuries. That way, one can avoid malicious remarks concerning the tributes paid by the country's first capital to her latest successor. Greetings to you too, Rio de Janeiro. From the ex-First Lady to the ex-Second Lady. In all sincerity.

Calunga, assigned to cover the unusual expedition, was issued with battle fatigues, snake-proof boots, a canteen and an identity disk to pin on his breast: *Lieutenant-journalist.* When he returned he was on the front pages. And he earned a medal.

Whether with or without speech I just can't remember. But I do remember that he chose the filthiest dive in town to celebrate the winning of his lofty distinction.

Like a good soldier: in the red-light district.

Ex-drunk.

And ex many other things I prefer not to remember at the moment.

Calunga: Carlos Luna Gama.

He had a portrait of Ernest Che Guevara on his wall. And he drank himself to death.

Make yourself at home, cousin. The house is yours. But please, couldn't you perhaps stop banging that damned drum?

Two more hours. The time it takes to see a cinema or a theatre. Enough to go from Rio de Janeiro to Bahia, or Paris to London, by plane, and still have a good few minutes to spare. Half an hour more than a football game. A fantastic amount of time. Will it be enough to cure a hangover?

That is something the alarm clock won't be able to answer. But it will tell me the exact time to brush my teeth, shave, soap my carcass, give it a good scrubbing, wash my face, wash my carcass in the most antiseptic bath I ever was in, and swallow down a whole bottle of water and a glass of milk and a fruit juice of some sort. Afterwards, fine, you'll be ready for the daily grind, just knot a tie round your neck and get into the fray. Exactly two hours from now. With or without little coffins.

Seems they decided to leave me alone. I can hardly believe it. Bit by bit, they are fading away, like images on an out-of-focus video. Bye-bye, eh? Have a good trip. Go for a great march across the Central Plateau of Brazil. Chief Calunga knows where that is. According to what they say, there is a surfeit of authorities out there, but to offset that there are no corners and no traffic signs. And the walls are very modern. Still spanking new. And there's space, lots of space: it's a children's paradise. Go out into the streets. The squares. The squares belong to the people, just like the sky is for the airplane. Get into gear and take a short trip to Washington, DC, USA. Bye-bye. *Good luck.* Give us a ring, via Embratel. But not, not ever at five in the morning, okay?

3

On stage: a poet.

Spanish.

Name: Federico García Lorca.

Just look at that. Great happenings on my wall. It's a smash hit!

Bienvenido, señor Lorca.

What are you going to sing?

> FEDERICO GARCIA LORCA:
> *The children sing*
> *in the peaceful evening;*
> *clear stream,*
> *tranquil spring!*
>
> THE CHILDREN
> *How is your divine*
> *heart in joyousness?*
>
> ME
> *Bells tolling*
> *far away in the mist.*

4

That angels are light I knew already. That sinners are heavy, I knew that too. That the dead do not take orders from the living, I also suspected. But that they can generate a pocket of resistance, that I have just this minute discovered. The black coffin stayed.

The heavy bier has just taken up residence right in the middle of my wall. And looking as if it had always been nailed to it - and by my own hands.

Like a portrait of a loved one, a picture, an ornamental knick-knack, an image not yet lost in time. Like a household item. A piece of old furniture.

Our Lady of Perpetual Succour, save me!

It's like the poet said:

"No head can bear so much reality."

Nor such a hangover.

Rio de Janeiro, oooh
Rio de Janeiro, eeeh
Rio de Janeiro
What a place to beee.

To put it in plain language: who might be this unexpected visitor, cased in black, who invades my bedroom so unceremoniously and who waits, impassively, for me to decipher him?

Hello, hello. Hi. Good morning. Might I know who is there?

Nobody's ghost, doc. Keep cool. It's just a shadow. Light reflected on the curtain. A pale invasion of daylight.

Wish it were. My children, I can see it, you bet, with my wide-open unsleeping eye. And there can't be any possibility of doubt: it really is a coffin. Black as black can be. This exotic visitor of mine could have had the kindness to let me know he was coming. That way I would have got ready to welcome him. With a crucifix, incense, a rosary and loads of holy water.

Hello, hello. Our telephones work now, without cables and all, did you know? Our posts and telegraphs are now into the age of information technology. Would it have been any trouble to let me know you were coming?

Splendid. Spokesman from the Beyond assaults Copacabana apartment. Believe me if you will. And imagine the panic. If the population is already locking itself in behind three and four locks, alarms, electronic janitors and all sorts of useless paraphernalia, to protect itself against the living, how will it react when this piece of news leaks out and goes from mouth to mouth? The police, quite rightly, will fold their arms. The matter is outside their jurisdiction. To whom to appeal then? To God?

Children, don't make a noise. Silence. God is asleep. While he sleeps the sleep of the just, I, sinner, confess that I can't get a wink. To Him, the dreams. To me, the hangover, the alarm clock and the shoot-out in the hillside slum, right next to my ear. And the little blue coffins, and the black coffin. Would I be making an awful nuisance of myself if I were to phone God, now? Press the button (your automatic pilot) and switch off. Relax. Try to sleep. You need it.

You are in need of a survival manual, with all the exercises for moments of tension. You need to attain the weightlessness possible in levitation. Go into a foam orbit and ride the rainbow. Sleep. Dream. Maybe it's a simple matter of switching channels. Switch from black-and-white to colour and from night to day. Change the scenario. By blending, cutting, superimposing, or by some other technological trick, it doesn't matter. Allow yourself to roll that scene filmed by the Spaniard, Carlos Saura, the one that excited you so in the cinema and which always excites you when you remember it. What was the film called? Must have been *Momma Turns a Hundred.* You could never forget the moment when a woman (Geraldine Chaplin, no doubt) walks towards the camera, opening and closing a long coat, under which she wore nothing, only her quite naked, magnificently exciting body. Seduction of seductions: she is walking towards her brother-in-law! She wants him. She desires him. She is letching for him. Opening her coat: - Sí? Closing it: - No?

Yes? No? Yes? No?

There are drunks who, in an advanced stage of alcoholism, start seeing monstrous spiders on the walls, crawling towards them. The so-called hallucinating visions. They are said to be terrifying. Shall I be lucky enough to hallucinate sufficiently to see Geraldine Chaplin's spider, or any other of the same class, coming in my direction? Sí? No? Sí? No? Did I say spider? A beautiful pussy in urgent need of being impaled. (At this point, a patriotic protest from the national *macho:* "What's this then, friend? After all, what are these imported scarecrows compared to our latest stable of fillies, nurtured on goat's milk, and which, at this time of the morning, are just beginning to prance around on the Rio beaches to keep in form, tummies in, bottoms out? *Relax and enjoy it.*")

Yes? No? Yes? No?

"Not nice, man."

Heavy rock gets louder then softer in BG. That

means "background", in this case, musical.

FM is already on the air. All bright-eyed and bushy-tailed, the FM also wakes up early.

Announcer:

"Never mind then! Keep it cool, partner. The main thing is to look up, morale high. Always cheerful. Rio de Janeiro goes on being beautiful. My, your, our Rio. Smile. Today the beach will be a winner. Get in the swim. The crowd there is in for a heatwave. Don't stay in an astral trough. The cool big sound you are about to hear is for you to have a ball with a really cuddly kitten. The good time."

Rock gets louder. Explosion of sound.

I'd like to see you sleep with a noise like this.

My God.

God, God, God.

Do you exist? Then help me. Do you love me, do you want me, do you call me a child of God?

SOS. Help. SOS. Help.

For God's sake.

Give me a proof of Your existence. Time is short.

And tell me, explain to me, make clear to me, enlighten me: who will pay the ransom demanded by the shades? Between the dead weight of the past and the uncertainties of the future, what am I to do with my ghosts? Lastly, but not finally (and to be even clearer): who is it really inside that coffin? Why has he come and what does he want from me?

First hypothesis:
MOMMA

"Hi, how're you? Everything alright with you, old girl?"

Go on, Mother. Say:

"Where are your manners? Is that a way for a child to address his mother?"

Oh Mother, thy name is touchiness.

"But what did I do wrong?"

(I have to add: "Don't hit me. I swear I haven't done anything.")

"Just watch yourself! Show me respect. Don't you ask my blessing?"

"Your blessing, Momma."

"God bless you, m'son."

That's better: back to square one.

"How are things? What's the news, Mother?"

"That's what I want to know. What have you to tell me?"

"The only real news is bad news. Joe the pharmacist has died."

"Is that true? Did he die of old age? How did it happen? Was he killed or did he just die?"

"That I don't know."

"Poor Joe. Such a good man. He spent his life

77

fighting death for other people. A fine soul."

"Seems you've forgiven him then."

"But what did the poor fellow ever do to me?"

"Arrived too late."

"I'll tell you how things happened, so that you can stop having evil thoughts about our pharmacist."

"It was people who said awful things about him, Mother. I was a boy but I remember very well. They said: 'Worthless character. Posing as a doctor and all he is is a butcher.' "

"Is that what they said about him? Well I'll tell you. My death started in the middle of the night and you know how long the nights were back home. Your father made me cups of tea, one after another, but it was no good. So then he went out into the field and got up on a mule that was worse to ride than need be. We lived a good bit off the road, remember? Your father, what with his lame leg, poor man, the leg that was shorter than the other, off he goes on an ass slower than a tortoise. And me there giving up the ghost."

"He had a gammy leg but he stuffed twenty-four kids in your belly. Of course the time had to come when you'd say: 'I give up.' "

"Don't be so impudent, you young puppy. Listen to the story. So while I was fainting away with pain, your father was spurring the mule and the road getting farther and farther away. 'Wake up, Joe. Run Joe. Find a horse for Joe. Quick, for

God's sake,' and me slipping away. If there wasn't even time for me to bless you and your brothers and sisters for the last time, how do you think the poor pharmacist could have made it in time to save me? Joe the pharmacist was in no way to blame."

"Oh those bad old days."

"Don't complain, m'son. I actually had a liking for those days of yore. My flowers in the back yard, mmmmm, so sweet smelling. The wind in the banana trees. The smell of rosemary in that sun-drenched wilderness. And lots of children, lots of children. One a year. That's life."

"Talking of children, you passed away, Mother, but your last baby survived."

"It was a miracle of God. Wasn't it?"

Sure. It was. Must have been. Don't ask me.

A baby every year and clothes to make, masses of clothes to wash. A baby every year and the yard to sweep and the house to clean and beans to plant, pick, riddle and sort and put on the fire to cook and the corn to strip and the pestle to pound and the cassava to scrape and the grater to turn and the pressed cassava to crumble and .the kids' hair to cut and their heads to delouse. A baby every year and the little angels to bury and the girls who are nearly old enough to get married already and the boys who are already starting to study. One every year. How can a woman bear one after another until she reaches the round sum of two dozen? Two dozen people, a nestful, like they were chickens. Give birth, bear and go on bearing until she dies.

Giving birth.

I remember that night. Nobody could get any sleep. I was ten years old and, as always, I was snuggled in a hammock among a heap of kids. It was always the same. When father came in with the midwife, we, the small fry, snuggled together in expectant silence, like on stormy days, which required every bit of respect for the Lightning God and Our Lord Thunder. Little though we were and unable to understand what are said to be the mysteries of life, we already knew that a woman could die in childbirth. Only when father crossed the room in the direction of the yard, with a dozen rockets in his hand to inform the world of the new arrival (yet another member of the family), did we go back to being children, heartened by the new baby's cry: another one to join the ring, another one to play with. But that night the midwife didn't deliver the goods (she would have to do without her usual payment, a litre each of beans and flour, and a bottle of rum) and Joe the pharmacist, called in haste, failed to arrive in time. That night there were no rockets. Only tears. And early next morning the house was full of flowers, but they did not smell like flowers, they smelt like death. And a lot of people came, from a long way away, to weep as well or to make sad faces. And all other sounds were subdued by the rough music of a saw followed afterwards by the hard knocking of nails. My father said: "This time Our Lady of Easy Births did not give her a good time. God willed it so. Resign yourselves." He scowled, but didn't cry, and didn't say another word.

"She is in God's hands now," said one of us. "And the girl, our little sister, is in the world's hands. In our hands."

They tried to close my mother's eyes because they said that a dead person must not go to her grave with her eyes open. Old superstitions, with little or no explanation. Must be fear that the deceased might be watching us. The only thing I couldn't be resigned to was the expression and the colour of my mother's face. It looked like wax. Where was the pretty smile that used to spread over her dark round face, electrifying her jet black hair which flowed down over her shoulders? What had happened to her bouncy thickset body - always pregnant - and her skin that was burnt and toughened by the blazing sun? Why had the sparkle faded in her cherry-black eyes? Once upon a time there was a genuine Indian woman with the purest native blood, we could say from the depths of our grief, were it not for the fact that Indians do not belong to our current point of reference, being nothing more than faded pictures in books at the country school which only a few attended. For us the world was divided entirely into blacks and whites, and to be white it was enough to have *good* hair like my mother's.

And she always had something nice to give us. The most incredible sweets. The most fantastic mealy pap. Only tasty things that had us licking our lips and asking for more.

And now? What do I have to offer her? Not even a hammock for her to rock her sins to sleep in and let her poor tired old soul fly away. After all, I do live in the most beautiful city in South America, maybe the most beautiful city in all the Americas - in the world! My mother will surely be breathless at all this beauty and there I'd be singing sweet and low in her ear, with my toneless, tuneless voice:

> *Rio de Janeiro*
> *I love you*
> *I love those who love*
> *this sky*
> *this sea*
> *these happy folk.*

If I were one of those sons with whom no Mother could find fault, I would have her kneel at the feet of Christ the Redeemer, on the top of the Corcovado mountain. Surely a Jesus Christ that size she never saw even in heaven. And when she turns her back on Him and looks towards the city, I guarantee that there's no view like that even in Paradise. Then there's the Sugar Loaf Mountain (I just hope she doesn't feel dizzy when she gets on the tramcar), from where she will get absolute proof that if God made the world in seven days, one whole day was devoted to making this city.

It's going to be hard telling her that I won't have time to go with her on this wonderful excursion. Worse still: how am I going to explain that to this day I do not know a single one of those places of such renown in prose, verse and postcard? Here, all I do is work, old girl. I toil. From time to time I go on a bender, of course, nobody's made of iron.

Such is life.

That's right, Dona Maria, have the kindness not to ask me about the *others*. The honest-to-goodness truth is I don't know a thing about them. How so, if, as their brother, I had an obligation to know? God will never forgive me? Let alone you, of course, Mother. How can I justify such an enormous failing? Please, don't condemn me too hastily. If you don't already know it, the time has come for you to be told that, the moment they were old enough, all your children hotfooted it into the big bad world - scattered all over the place. I mean the lucky ones who escaped the little blue coffin, though I'm not sure if it was luck or misfortune. You only need to count: twenty-four less two. And those twenty-two no sooner put on their first long trousers than they discovered that Brazil is huge, full of roads and promises. And I don't have the time or the money to travel around in search of them, one by one, just to ask: "How goes it?" just to be answered "Okay, so-so, and how're things with you?"

In spite of my lack of interest for your numerous offspring, I still hope for a much greater kindness from you, Mother: don't ask me about the guy who popped twenty-four kids into your belly, the gent with the limp who turns out to be my father. I don't know whether he's alive or dead either. If he died nobody remembered to let me know. I visited him one day, a long time ago, taking my children to meet him. I found him holed up in a miserable shack at the entrance to a deserted hamlet. This is what I saw: an old man, a horse, a dog and a bottle of hooch. And that was all that was left of my world. He went crazy (much more than he already was) when he saw the children, his "grandchildren from Rio". In no time he rushed off to the nearest field, invaded a house and returned with a chicken under his arm, which he skinned and plucked, rapidly proceeding to serve us the best lunch in the world. I gave him some money, a bag full of clothes and promised that I would go back again before long. And that was all I saw. A man all by himself, either by decision, conviction or for some other inscrutable reason, and wholly dependent on some good soul taking him a plate of food from time to time, his kindly old neighbours from previous times who had not altogether forgotten him. And this person, who was once my father and whom I tried to recognize as such, now looked a mere shadow of his former self, starting with his size. I imagined him much stiffer - despite his having one leg just that bit shorter than the other - and much more powerful. I'm not just referring to the virile character who gave the world twenty-four children of his making (twenty-four delights and three deaths, including yours, Momma, twenty-four problems, twenty-odd civil servants), but to the man who was able to build his own house, the house in which I was born, with his own hands. And it was a huge house, with lots of verandahs, sunny windows, store-room and pantry, a corral close by and a shed where the flour was kept, as an addition. The lord of all these domains was alone and far from everything - the house, the corral, his children. Nothing now existed, as if nothing had existed before. Neither the yard where I learned to play, nor the creek where I learned to swim. Nor the fig tree by the door, nor the jujube next to it, nor the cherimoya, the custard apple and the cashew trees at the back. Nor the flower garden, nor the banana orchard. From up there, from that hole he was stuck in, I could conclude, without fear of error, that nothing was as I had cherished it in the realm of my imagination. I wanted to tell my three children, those three products of the tarmac:

"Look there. Do you see? Well, I was brought up there, running wild all day long, not afraid of ghosts. While you three, just to cross the road where we live, have to hold onto my trouser belt

85

and my hands."

There was nothing to see, nothing to say. Everything was far away, tiny and destroyed. There was nothing else there except an old man and a shack, way in the distance, way beyond my own remoteness. Where should I find my own time? In a lost hole on the edge of life more than a thousand miles away, goodness knows how many light years away from me. And yet the man - this shrivelled, decaying old man, this gentleman who had once been my father - was still able to reconcile me to that time, just by taking three sprigs of rosemary and putting one behind the ear of each of my children. And saying:

"This is against the evil-eye. It's to protect you all from evil. You are lovely children."

As we were leaving, the unexpected happened, something I couldn't foresee and didn't want to happen. It was enough to cut one's heart in a thousand pieces. He began to sing, as if he were the happiest man on earth. He dug into his memory for old cowboy calls and songs of yore and sang them with idiotic happiness, like a madman, a man on good terms with life. And his voice followed along the road:

> *Weep banana tree,*
> *banana tree weep.*
> *Weep banana tree,*
> *because today's the day*
> *I go away.*

And I was thinking: he can die here any moment and no one will even notice. Who will make his coffin? And who will carry him to his grave?

Weep banana tree,
banana tree weep.

Why did you die, Momma? Why did you go and die, Mother? What for?

But even so, you don't need to stand there, stock-still and dumb as a post. Don't worry: your son is not some market researcher in the employ of one of our hundreds of specialized corporations, national or foreign.

Well? Don't you want to know what work I do and what my employment is? I am in the business of wheelers and dealers. I am part of the fluid, alluring world of my era. I am one who has succeeded, by his own efforts and merit, in penetrating the innermost secrets of a thrillingly modern professional class. I repeat: by merit and effort. Though I must add, on the side of truth: also with a bit of a shove from Lady Luck. Hold on to your hat, Momma, 'cos I'm going to tell you exactly what I am. An ADSWEFA. Steady on, don't worry, I'll translate: AD - for Adviser. SWE - for Sweet. FA - for Fuck All. Adviser for Sweet Fuck All. An occupation, despite its odd name, relatively highly priced in the market. In order to occupy such a position, one has to be reasonably educated, needs to know how to dress, have a flexible waist, and gossamer lips so as to be able to suck up to one's clients without leaving a trace. Good taste is fundamental. Whether in the choice of drinks or in the use of the correct cutlery to accompany each dish. A good handbook of quotations, duly memorized, is also important. The right joke, the right sentence, even the right piece of verse at the right moment are important contributions to one's professional development in this sphere. All this plus a smile of smug ignorance. And lots of perspicacity, charm and Vaseline. Ah, Mother, Vaseline has so increased in value. Nowadays it is a hotly contested commodity, due to its excellent qualities: it makes things move smoothly. Put that way, hastily, it all seems very easy. But it isn't. There are other secrets that we have to discover as we plod along. And what do you think of it all, Mother? Living off ballyhooland is one hell of a strain. It exhausts, tires, vexes, and causes ulcers, heart attacks and cancer. The worst is that lately the market has been rather debased by an excessive availability of gab artists, which causes our price to fall a good deal. That law of supply and demand, have you heard of it? Well, it's because of it that I travel every day to the firm where I work, not knowing if I've been dropped already. You have to agree, it gives one an unbearable pain in the guts. You need strong nerves. Believe me, Momma. An Adswefa has a head and a heart too. Adswefas are human. Why the expression of disgust, old lady? Are you feeling unwell? Are you going to vomit? Do you want some fruit salts? A glass of sugar water? What was it? Wait a bit. Don't go yet. Let's talk. Have you brought me some magic money? I know, I know. Magic money, buried gold, that was in olden times. Old beliefs. Sheer illusion. Nowadays, no one who has money is silly enough to hide it in the earth, like they say people used to do in earlier times. Nowadays the cash goes straight to the bank. In Switzerland. Okay Momma, money ain't everything. (Fine phrase.) But what on earth am I going to do with all these little blue coffins? Do you by any chance know where they come from and where they are going? Yes, yes. Innocent little angels going up to heaven. (Another very beautiful phrase.) And heaven is already full to capacity. And they need care and shelter until some more vacancies are created up there, isn't that it? They are knocking on the wrong door. It's no good here. The apartment is small, you can see that, Mother. Lounge and three bedrooms. What? Who's going to keep the boat afloat? How should I know?

Please, Momma. Tell me you love me. Say: "God keep you." Go on, Mother. Say it.

Amen.

Second hypothesis:
AUNT MADALENA, CALUNGA'S MOTHER

This is how I remember her: an obstinate steadfast woman, with great tenacity, who always knew what she wanted. She went through some hard times in her life, but unlike my mother (her elder sister) not always by doing heavy work. Of course, she had the good fortune to have had only one child, a measure which we can now interpret as proof of the greatest wisdom - although we never discovered whether it was by her own decision or due, let's say, to a whim of destiny. In her day, however, it was viewed as out and out quirkiness. A woman was really meant to bring forth, to have litters, like bitches and she-cats. Bring forth with a will. Be born, grow up and die bringing forth. Like my mother. Was Aunt Madalena perhaps ill-fated?

Suppositions were ventured. People speculated. Might she be prey to some secret sorrow or was it her drunkard of a husband who was not doing his job properly: having fallen in love with a bottle, he no longer did justice to his well-appointed property - that blessed pair of breasts and thighs? Might she be living in sin, succumbing, with the aid of the pharmacist, to the remedies to avoid having children which it was beginning to be said now existed?

The only sin she never committed was lack of objectivity. She changed her abode - and direction - as often as she thought necessary. Very early, and to our amazement, she discovered that a woman can also work on her own account, without needing to spend the rest of her life at a man's expense. When she became a widow, she did not have the patience to wait for the official period of mourning to finish - a year! - before hitching up with another man, which she did without asking any judge for a receipt or any priest for his blessing. And she begged nobody's pardon when she decided to swap men again. She was not exactly a disgrace. She was simply difficult to convince. This earned her some rather unflattering descriptions: headstrong, bossy, high and mighty. A hard nut. She was capable of undertaking long "business" trips all by herself, just imagine. And yet, if her obstinacy gave her a certain practical sense about life, it still didn't make her a bitter woman. Quite the reverse: if my Aunt Madalena did not give the immediate impression of being an affable, amusing, funny person, neither could one say that she was an unredeemable bore. One way or another, she always lent a willing ear to those who knocked on her door. And, let's face it, her relatives were an impecunious gang who were always turning to her for assistance, a regular heartbreak chorus. To do her justice, she never denied a glass of water, a plate of food and a chat to anyone who pitched up at her house at any hour of the day or night. However, if gratitude is the reward for effort, it is difficult to know if she ever felt satisfied. What I do know is that her extreme tenacity hardened her character and made her impervious to subtleties. As her son Calunga knew only too well. But that's another story.

This is how I see her: giving orders, pushing others forward, swearing at the lazy ones, cursing the drunkards and the good-for-nothings. She see-med to have been born to command: she was a typical representative of the northeastern matriar-chy. A born sergeant-major.

What's the order, old lady? Looking for your son?

I regret to inform you that he no longer lives on this planet.

But this you knew already, of course.

It was you who did him the kindness of burying him, was it not?

You mean to say it was me that led him astray?

Steady on, madam. I only had the odd drink with him, here and there.

Have you anything to tell me? Something I never knew or suspected?

Be so good as to step out of that coffin and show yourself. Make yourself at home. And you can be absolutely sure that I have never forgotten you, you who were a mother to me. You brought me up, sent me to school, even sewed the occasional button on my shirts. How could I forget you? Can you tell me what you're here for, what I can do for you, what complaints you have? Some disappointment? Come on, Auntie, tell me. Tell me all. Don't hide anything. Are you missing this old world? Up there in the renowned Beyond, is it better or worse than here?

What I hope for: that she has brought wild flowers to cheer up my house and my life. That she still has good memories of this nephew of hers. That she will talk to me. That her voice does not have the slightest trace of resentment, hate, sadness or disappointment. And that she can still smile and will smile at me and her smile will be a revelation: that happiness exists, here on earth as in heaven. That she will bring me fresh exciting news. That, like the excellent gossip she is, she will tell me the latest news about God and thereabouts.

So:

"I've seen him, boy, with these eyes that the worms have already eaten. God is naked. Marvel! But I've also discovered that the angels do have sexes and that they live in eternal debauchery, in a perennial state of celestial whoredom. They are all dying because of a very strange epidemic, an extremely odd disease called AIDS, which no God can find a cure for. As for the devil, didn't you

93

know? Oh, don't tell me you didn't know! He was beheaded, ruthlessly, by our outlaw Virgulino Ferreira, that wicked Lampião. First he had the devil singing that song that went 'Maria Bonita wake up / and get the coffee warming / 'cause now the dawn is come / and the police they are aswarming,' for his gang to dance to three days and three nights, non-stop. They say it was one hell of a rave-up, the biggest shindig of all time, a great rumpus. What a romp. Hell's last ball. Lampião's outlaws were completely drunk and frenzied, ready to tear the place apart. Poor Satan pulled all sorts of dreadful faces, went down on his knees, asked for help, pleaded for the love of God and all the saints, said he couldn't stand it, all that whistling, complained he'd lost his tweet, that his jaws ached, that he had no more puff.

"And Lampião: '*Play it again, Sam.* Ain't you Sam? Of course you're Sam. Y'old devil. *Play it again, Sam.*' After three days and three nights of revelry with hell reduced to a wreck, Lampião the outlaw took his Bowie-knife to the devil's privates, slicing them off as calmly and coolly as a man castrating an ox. When the job was done, he held up the devil's balls in triumph for his gang to see and said:

" 'Right! This one won't be fucking people up no more. *Never more.*' "

Another victory for our colours. Shattering. There's the proof: nobody can hold us. It's Brazil going all out. Crushing the opposition - goals galore. Even in hell. And I thought that only big brothers Jesse and Frank James, the Dillingers, the Billy the Kids and that nice couple Bonnie Parker and Clyde Barrow would be capable of such an extraordinary feat. A big hand for our outlaw Lampião, a great guy. Brazil for ever. Come on, gang:

"Oh, oh, oooh, Brazil. Another one, Brazil!"

The sad thing, though, is that the avenging spirit of the King of Outlaws has not come down in these parts for a long time. It really is a pity, because we are very much in need of a macho guy to slice the balls off a whole lot of whoresons who're fucking up our lives. Don't tell me even the spirit of Lampião has died? What? He's swapped his shooting iron and his Bowie-knife for a guitar and an electronic synthesizer, banditry for rock'n'roll? Shocking, sister. Tell me more, tell me all, Auntie. Don't hide anything. What? Why don't the living come out fighting, instead of sitting by the roadside waiting for a Saviour from the Stone Age to come back to life and push them up onto the truck that will take them to Paradise? I sure don't know. They say it's laziness, starvation, disorder and fear. But do you believe that Paradise exists? What great news. Tell it to everybody, Auntie.

One, two, three. All together now, gang:

I live-tum-tum-tum-
in a tropical land-tum-tum-tum-

blessed by God-tum-tum-tum-
and a pretty sight.
Skibum-dum-dum-
Oh what a beautiful sight!

What I hope for from my unforgettable Aunt Madalena: that she's come to point to the exact piece of Brazilian soil where I can dig and find a chest full of magic money.

I want to make clear, Auntie, that I'm not prepared to waste time running after a piddling little chest lined with the petty cash of those mean Jesuit priests from the time of King John Hornhead, or with the paltry *milreis* of tight-fisted ranchers, which worried our forefathers so much, making them lose their sleep dreaming of wandering souls, in the hope that they would come and tell them the exact spot where the chest had been hidden.

No, I have no wish to turn into a collector of old coins and legends.

Nor is it your sweated small change, dear Aunt, that I'm after.

I know that your modest patrimony was divided up in equal parts among your grandchildren, who must have squandered it all on icecreams and gum.

I'm modern, that I am. Don't come here with any old money.

I want MONEY. US dollars. None of your Canadian.

Hell, Auntie, has no bored foreign ambassador

decided to hang himself, but not before first magnanimously taking care to bury his treasure chest in national soil, right under my nose? What? This business of hanging oneself is one of our tricks? What a pain. Shit. Merde, alors. It's not possible there are no other ways. You only need to follow the trail of certified wealthy compatriots who, on declaring themselves bankrupt, squeezed the trigger against their own brains. Might they not, minutes before carrying out the insane act, have lodged in our soil the last of their chests destined for their numbered Swiss bank accounts? We need to act quickly, my adored aunt, before a hundred or so million vultures get wind of this precious carrion. Down to work, Aunt Madalena.

What I do NOT hope for from her:

That she's already shaking her head from side to side in a mixture of astonishment and commiseration.

That she will say:

"Poor boy. You still believe in the existence of enchanted money. I guess you still believe in Santa Claus and the life eternal too. It's easy to see that you're drunk. Your breath stinks from miles away. It's like I always said: drink softens the brain, it leaves any man with a screw loose. Drink is man's ruin."

Didn't I say that she wasn't much given to certain subtleties?

I've seen everything: my esteemed, sadly missed,

dearest, kind Aunt Madalena has not brought me any flowers.

Even so, I have to accord her all the honours of the house, with pomp and circumstance - fireworks and fanfares, a loaded table and assorted liqueurs. You know what our relatives are like, don't you? The least little oversight and they feel unwanted. The more so when it's a relative one hasn't seen for a long time. As for them, in the majority of cases, they're awfully touchy. We never know if we're really pleasing them. One has to be careful so that they don't go around afterwards making the host a laughing-stock.

To make my aunt feel really at home here - despite having arrived without prior notice - and for her to realize right away how welcome she is, how I revere her, how much I love her, how grateful I am to her for past favours, I shall have to start by celebrating her arrival in a suitable manner. I want to have the pleasure of seeing her shake from head to foot at the eloquence of my greeting - the unambiguous proof that I have never forgotten her and never will. In the best Bahian style, I shall search my memory (impromptu!) for a cool speech. Just to be sure of piercing her old heart I shall make mine the words of the poet Charles Baudelaire - of whom, I am quite sure, she has never heard. But, like a good Aunt (and a good Bahian!) she doubtless still appreciates pretty words, spoken with taste and charm. My aunt will roll her eyes up and down with emotion when she hears this early morning orator, lyrical and tender, though dead drunk.

Therefore, it is with much love and affection that I dedicate to the lady cased in black on my wall this lovely page from my private repertoire:

GET DRUNK

One should always be drunk. It all comes down to this; that is the only problem. So as not to feel the dreadful burden of Time, which exhausts you and weighs you into the ground, you need to get drunk incessantly.

But on what? On wine, poetry or virtue, whichever you think best. As long as you get drunk.

And if sometimes, on the steps of a palace, on the green grass of a ditch, in the desolate loneliness of your room, you awake with your drunkenness already diminished or gone, ask of wind, wave, star, bird or clock, of everything that flees, moans, rolls, sings or speaks, ask them what time it is; and the wind, and the wave, and the star, and the bird, and the clock shall answer you:

"It is the hour of drunkenness! Do not be the martyred slaves of Time. Get drunk; get drunk without respite! On wine, poetry or virtue, whichever you prefer."

Did you like that, Auntie? Not at all? So so? I know, you prefer Castro Alves. Antonio de Castro Alves, poet of Bahia. Is this preference of yours sheer parochialism or is it just a matter of taste? Of course, of course, tastes are not open to question. What? That was the really good one? THAT:

> *Vert-aureate flag of my homeland dear,*
> *brushed and blown by breezes from Brazil.*
> *Banner which in thee enfold'st the sunlight*
> *clear,*
> *and the promises divine that hope instils...*

Come on, Auntie, only a character in a lamentable state of total sobriety, without a single drop of alcohol in his veins, could have written a thing like that. Because the truth is this, dear Aunt: only drunkards see the world go round.

Talking of which, you didn't bring me a drop of rum from up north in that coffin of yours, did you? The real McCoy, made in a clay still? Nothing better than a good drop of rum, as a pick-me-up. It livens up the brain. I know: you didn't bring any. No rum, no dried meat, no tapioca cake, no coconut butter, no raw candy. Ungrateful old woman.

"Ungrateful yourself, you never even took me to McDonald's."

Step forward. Make yourself at home. You're welcome. Let's have a talk.

Like in the old days, when you had the stamina to be the last one out of the last bar, from which you sometimes went straight to work. How did you manage to keep going? But you did. And you even used to say that you had your whole life ahead of you for sleeping. Why bother?

Have you been sleeping well? What do you think of the much proclaimed eternal rest? Is it really restful? A splendid cradle?

Did you know that your mother, my unforgettable Aunt Madalena, got angry with me for ever and ever?

All because I didn't go to your funeral. I just had to be the first to take up position as one of your pall bearers. And I didn't even send flowers. Nor did I take the trouble to write her a few moving lines. I could at least have sent a telegram or phoned to say something, anything, in a voice affected by my words of sympathy, every bit like a professional master of funeral ceremonies, a voice full of compassion, measured, against a background of sincere sobs, the engineered sound of grief for an irreparable loss:

"That's life, Auntie. Though I was expecting the news at any moment, and I'd been expecting it for years, and despite knowing just how much he'd been killing himself, although I thought he was standing it pretty good, yes, he went down fighting, didn't he? - and little as the news surprises me, even so, despite everything, I'm...I'm... (How *ought* I to be in fact? Sad? Empty?). No, Auntie, let us not mourn his death. After all he enjoyed himself a fair bit. And, when I think of it, he had a long life. Forty! Who'd have thought it, eh? Some life, for someone who started so early. Bravo for your big son. A round of applause for my big cousin. Please, send him a wreath from me, but sprinkle it with rum. Don't forget that detail. He deserves that memento."

"He was a brother to you. A real brother."

"That's exactly why I know that he doesn't want tears or candles now. They don't go with him. He's not the type. Put a nice bottle of something in his coffin, that's what he likes. But be careful. None of your fancy stuff. Either a real scotch whisky, or a genuine national product, aged in a clay still. It has to be a really fierce drink like whisky or rum. He drank the hard stuff."

"At least you'll come to the seventh day mass, won't you?"

"What mass, Auntie? Your son never set foot in a church."

"That's all I need. No seventh day mass. Have you gone out of your mind? What will people say? That I'm an unnatural mother, like they always said?"

"Has anybody offered to pay for the funeral? No? Well then. You don't have to be beholden to anybody."

"There shall be a mass, that there shall. That I cannot and will not do without. Will you come and see me? I'm so lonely!"

And your husband? (She was never without one and each was more cussed than the one before.) And your daughter-in-law? And your grandchildren? And your goodness knows how many sisters? And your gang of relatives and hangers-on? The family is endless. Why should you be feeling lonely?

But then, I couldn't forget that she'd been my mother's best sister. She promised to take me and put me to study and she kept her promise. As soon as my mother died, she went and fetched me, took me away to another town, saved me from being an orphan. She had only one child, she could afford to bring up another. Wasn't it just that I should now go and see her? She was my favourite aunt. I hadn't the slightest doubt about that.

"Promise you'll come soon?"

There she was in Bahia and me in Rio de Janeiro. More than a thousand miles away.

"As soon as I can, Aunt Madalena. Right now I

can't, unfortunately. I really would like to rush up and see you. But believe me, just now I can't. I'm so busy, got so much work."

"Come on, take a break, take a holiday. Come and see me. I'm waiting."

Friendly Bahian families. They adore getting visits. Particularly from people who live far away and might arrive from one moment to the next bringing lots of news. The door will always be open and the table ready to be laid. Today there'll be pork and beans, *caruru, vatapá,* pig's-liver hash or whatever.

"Bring the pepper, girlie."

Yes, well. I don't know what happened but I never had the courage to so much as give my aunt a phone call. She must have waited for it for the rest of her life. And she certainly died without ever forgiving me. And I should have telephoned, to tell the naked truth:

"Don't get uptight, Auntie. All he really wanted was to die. He eventually succeeded. What can we do? Miss him. That's all. Nothing else."

And you? What are you doing there in this little black coffin? Come to pester me?

Easy on there. I'll tell you how it all happened.

Do you still remember the panic caused by a telephone ringing by your bedside at four in the morning?

I knew it was four in the morning because before I answered I saw the number gleaming brightly on the dial of the digital radio alarm. *Made in Paraguay* or *Made in Japan.*

"Excuse me if I woke you up," said the voice at the other end. "But your best friend has died."

"And you call me at this hour?"

"Well, I've just been woken up as well. Since the funeral is at eleven o'clock, I thought if I let you know now you'd still have time to go to the airport and catch a plane."

"Fine time you chose to call me, didn't you? Get lost."

"Anyway, you've been informed." And he rang off.

What should I do?

To start with, I'd just made myself an enemy.

The character who woke me up, when he realized that I hadn't liked it one little bit, banged the phone down in my ear. Touchy, eh? He must have thought he was doing his duty. He was naturally disappointed by my...by my...by my what? Coldness? Indifference? Rudeness? Come on, mister Informer, renowned Angel of Death: I was just sinking into the best part of my sleep. I was actually dreaming, you know. When the telephone rang, I was not the only one who got a shock. My wife (Cris to her friends) woke up as well, complaining. And while I was answering the call, she was asking:

"Who is the crazy fool?"

And afterwards, when I hung up, she insisted:

105

"Who was it? Hell, is that a time to phone anybody?"

I answered:

"Calunga's dead."

And she:

"Poor Calunga."

And she mumbled one or two more aimless phrases, made less than clear by sleep. It seemed she wanted to say something, but didn't know what. Cris had seen you at close quarters on some of your worst days. She thought you'd given it all up a long time ago. Nothing more to do. She considered you a good person, a great friend. And she said it was such a pity to watch you going downhill like that. And she would ask me: "How come? What happened to him? What's his problem?"

Cris managed to go back to sleep. Her sleep was stronger than the bad news.

Me, I got up, went to the lounge, found me a pack of cigarettes and waited for the dawn to break. Sitting there. Smoking. Thinking. Rambling.

And seeing you. On the walls, on the ceiling, either sitting opposite me or walking up and down the lounge, restless, shaking, rubbing your hands together. And saying:

"Isn't there a drink to be had in this house?"

My God. Hadn't you had your fill already? Why didn't you rest in peace?

But you kept on:

"Come and have just one more with me. At the graveside, fuck you."

And why not?

A few chords on the guitar would make this awkward moment more pleasant. It was your favourite instrument. And it was good to know that even now you hadn't given it up. Music, maestro. The occasion requires music. Music is superior to words, to silence, to everything.

"Let's see if I can remember," you said.

And you played:

> *No more*
> *No more than an illusion*
> *That's enough, darling,*
> *now it's too much for my*
> *heart.*

You stopped at that point. And laughed.

"Do you remember that?"

Not remember? You had actually done well in the competition for beginners in the "Voice of the Backlands" Loud-speaker Service. You even won a cake of Lifebuoy soap, to make you smell nice for the girls. A gift from the sponsor, the Primavera Store - "only the best articles, for men, women and children".

However, your success needled the rest of the class. The next day you were rewarded with a beating.

"And now, what are you going to sing?"

"Your arse."

Any day there wasn't a scrap after class was no fun. At last your turn had come.

The agitators were first-rate. They knew how to get a good fight going. They scored two circles on the ground with the toe of their shoe, then started the provocations, working the fighters into a fury:

"This here, look, is your mother. And this one here is his over there. Which of you is going to have the courage to be the first to step on the other's mother?"

You did it first. And you got a beating.

You'd never been in a scrap before. You took a real drubbing. Because you didn't know the first thing about fighting.

You got home with a black eye, a torn shirt and your face and arms covered in scratches. You had had your "baptism".

And you got another thrashing - from your mother. To make you stop fighting in the street like a hooligan.

"Now, Calunga, it's your turn," said the teacher.

Your legs quaked. Your hands were like ice.

A Brazilian flag in one hand. The other making gestures. You were reciting a poem by Castro Alves, Bahia's glorious poet! Your gestures were overdone for the poem. You were really very awkward.

"How talented!"

Vert-aureate flag of my homeland dear,
brushed and blown by breezes from Brazil.
Banner which in thee enfold'st the sunlight
clear,
and the promises divine that hope instils...

"It's nice to see."

The square was all decked out. In green and yellow. The dusty square was applauding you.

"That boy'll go far."

Was there anyone else there, apart from the schoolteacher, who knew the meaning of "vert-aureate"? Little matter. It was pretty, real pretty.

Some people said you had to go to the seminary and study to be a priest.

"He'll be this place's pride and joy."

Others thought it would be better for you to study for college. To be a college *lawyeer.*

And there were some, too, who saw an even more exalted destiny ahead of you: congressman. The adherents of this perspective could already see the day when you would mount the platform and give 'em hell, show them what you were made of:

"Fellow citizens."

And you went on reciting and gesturing.

"This poetry lark's girl's stuff. Or pansy's," said one of the boys from school. You went for him. But that scrap was cut short.

"Is it true, Calunga?"

109

"What?"

"That your father's going to sell everything he's got to send you to high school?"

"Go on. His father's leaving because he's drunk up all the rum there was here. There's not a drop left."

"That's not what they told me."

"What was it, tell us?"

"They're leaving because his father's going to see if he can get rid of his horns somewhere else."

"Is it true, Calunga? Your father's got a pair, has he? Must be hard having a father who's such a patsy. Real tough."

This time you took punishment but you handed it out as well. You laid in good and hard. You were savage.

"One by one. One at a time," said the ringleader.

You took them on, one after another. Foaming. Fuming. Bleeding. Kicking. Punching.

You left the square a hero. Admired and feared more than ever.

And your mother didn't give you a thrashing. She was sorry for you. You were cut all over. What you needed was to have your wounds seen to. And she must by now have known what the fight had been about. In that lousy dump everybody told everything to everybody. And you were dying to ask her:

"Is it true, Momma?"

But you'd fought like a trooper. You were pleased with yourself and couldn't care about anything else.

And you left almost immediately, on the back of a truck.

Your mother and father were in the cab.

You looked the happiest of the three.

A new place. A new life. A city. Even had a high school.

You were going to high school.

The truck travelled slowly, along a dirt road full of holes.

You, sitting on top of the freight, were leaving your old world behind. A few cows here and there, some sheep, some horses. Meadows. Cassava plots. A house with a verandah. A lime-washed cottage with a tree in the doorway. Banana orchards. And the sun, sinking in the west, gilding it all. It was a yellow sunset striped with red: a picture. Lovely. A strange feeling stirred inside you. What was it? Pain? Homesickness? The departure. You were leaving. For ever. The truck sounded its horn. "Onward, cries the numen in the soul," you recited, just for your own ears. But what was numen? What did it mean?

Castro Alves' poems had some very odd words in them.

Pom, pom,
prrom-pom-pom.

111

We are the boys
of the drunks' brigade,
ready to fall
in an all-night binge.

"Watch out, Calunga. The head. He's close by."

True soldiers are we
of our beloved country
cherished by her.

"He's at the end of the row now. Give us the navy one, the White Swan."

Like a headmaster who, on moonlit night,
went outside and crapped there in the light.

"The one about the soldier is better. It's got a better rhythm."

Rice we eat with beans, we do,
our rum we drink with lemon,
but when our dear land
has need of a shower
shitt'n hell we crap our ass-full.

Left, right, left, right.

Love red-hot
for dram and tot...

"Suspended for three days, master Calunga. And only because you're a good student. You have good marks. I've seen your report. But I won't have lack of discipline. Next time it'll be expulsion. Out on your ear. Make a note for a piece of

112

homework, so as not to be without something to do the next three days: to write the motto Order and Progress five hundred times. Easy, isn't it? It's just a tiny sentence. But there's another. Quotation marks. 'I love and respect all national anthems and symbols.' Close quotation marks. Five hundred times for that too."

You pocketed your pride and considered yourself very lucky. Just think, pupil no. 22, Carlos Luna Gama, what if the man decided to turn nasty and threw you out of high school? There's only this one, you know, Calunga. The only only one, just this high school. If you had been expelled, it'd have been the end of a career that was just starting. You were born lucky, man.

But where you were really lucky was that your mother either didn't notice or pretended not to notice your insistent stares, those very peculiar looks of yours at her legs. One day you actually confided to me:

"My mother has such a pair of thighs..."

I thought that was an odd thing to say. Nobody else said things like that about their mother. Even if they thought it, they'd just say nothing. Keep it secret. I thought: "This bastard's going screwy."

And you were on your way, straight to the whorehouse. Always finding a way of bumming some dough out of your mother, to pay for your women. You invented a thousand stories to squeeze the old girl. It was for the high school literary society, for this, that and the other. The great thing was your comradeship: there was occasionally some to spare for me as well. And the more often you went to the brothel, the more you stared at your mother's thighs. Your cadging from Aunt Madalena only lessened when a woman fell for you. Then you got it for free. Until you were branded with the clap, got scared and opted out. And who was going to pay for the penicillin injection? Why, of course, your mother's thighs. You felt unwell in the pharmacy, when you got the needle jab. You nearly fainted. The pharmacist got a fright and kept pushing your head down, then up again, saying: "Breathe deeply. In. Out."

The worst thing with gonorrhoea was when you wanted to piss. Standing there waiting, in front of the toilet, for the first drop and it coming hot, burning, hurting. That was when you saw stars. A torture. That wait for the first drop was like eternity. Just as well the penicillin worked quickly. What if you were allergic to penicillin? That sudden fainting feeling gave you quite a fright.

"Rifleman 27, attention! Fall out. Your father's dead. You've been sent for. Go home."

"Thank you, Sergeant."

"Scho-oo-l, attention! Fall out. Those who can should attend the funeral of 27's father."

You stopped by the first bar. You ordered a drink. You splashed the first mouthful on the ground. That was for the deceased. Then you tossed back the rest at one go, in honour of one who had died as he lived: drunk. You ordered a second. Your father deserved another tribute. You made it three and then decided: you wouldn't go home. What you'd do was go to the whorehouse. Why put up with your mother's tears and that whole distressing scene?

The one who had to play hostess to the deceased, and not set a foot outside all the way through his wake, was Aunt Madalena, no one else. Did she weep? And how! She wept and sobbed. Of course, some kindly souls from the neighbourhood appeared to help her with the arrangements. And your son? Isn't Calunga here? Hurry, go to the military training school. No one at the school, except a sentry, on duty at the door, standing stiffly at attention: looked like a lamp post. The corps had gone on a march to a training camp, a long away from headquarters. I left the message and rushed back. The living-room was by now full of flowers, surrounding the deceased. The sickly smell of those flowers was hard to endure. Some old women were praying in low voices. Others were seeing to coffee for the visitors. Time was going by. And Calunga? From time to time my aunt would raise her eyes and look in my direction. Every time she looked at me, I interpreted as follows:

1. Go and look for your cousin.

2. Why aren't you crying?

3. Go and look for your cousin.

4. Why aren't you crying?

And so on and so on.

She put these ideas across so many times through her wet, swollen eyes that I eventually left the house. First, though, I took one last look at the deceased. How he'd shrunk. What an ugly thing. He had died *suddenly,* sitting in his old rocking chair. It was all so quick, so peaceful. Dying like that couldn't be all that bad. There went the humble linen merchant, a man of few words, who loved music, liked to play the saxophone and who, as a boy, gave pleasure to many people, as a member of a church choir, at dances, at serenadings - would the surviving night owls come and play in his honour? He was a good soul. He had died as he had lived: without show or bluster. He left a dreadful reputation as a deceived husband, all because of a story made up, it was said, by a lousy scandal-monger, a rival shopkeeper who wanted to put him out of business. When the story got out on the streets, he found it convenient to make a move, and my aunt's advice was extremely influential in his decision. She knew her own mind. Had a head on her shoulders. She could make her presence felt, knew how to express just what she felt about things. The whole business was just a matter of envy, evil gossip, filth, baseness. A dirty trick.

"That does it. Let's get away. This place is a

dump. I can't stand any more," she said. "You can't so much as say good-day to a lousy bum without him thinking things and spreading lies. That's just too much."

And Calunga needed to go to high school. That place had no high school, no future, no nothing. It was time to move.

By local standards the move was unacceptable, unforgivable. What he was expected to do, as a man dishonoured, was grab his gun and avenge his honour by putting a hole straight through the blabbermouth's forehead. If he didn't, it meant he accepted the inevitable: the rumour was true.

"Not just a dupe, but impotent into the bargain."

But it was no time to remember such things.

I was only sorry I'd never talked to him properly, not known what he was really like, the way he thought. But after all I was just a kid and what importance can a youngster have for a man of his age? And he was an old man already, viewed from my age - what did he matter to me? There was only one occasion when he seemed to be interested in my existence. It was when he asked me to listen to a piece of music he was about to play. It was a bolero called *Those Green Eyes* that you heard all over the place, at any ordinary party, from every loud-speaker. But played by him, at that moment, on that solo saxophone, it sounded different, as if I'd never heard it before. I thought:

whose *Green Eyes* might they be? My aunt's eyes were as black as a raven's wing. I shuddered.

"Rest in peace, old sucker."

And I went off to kick a ball around with some kids, in a field a good long way away from the house. I just had to get well away from things for a time.

God only knows the complaints I had to listen to afterwards.

I should have more feeling, more consideration. Me and you, Calunga. You only turned up much later, holding yourself straight, avoiding conversation so that she shouldn't notice how drunk you were.

And it was no good explaining that I was frightened of the dead.

"He's your uncle. He was a father to you. And you, Calunga, how shameful, what bad manners. It's unforgivable."

We put our tails between our legs, made sad faces and had to go in the funeral procession.

My aunt was a hard woman.

"Rifleman 27, you're under arrest."

"Why, Sergeant?"

"Sergeant, sir. Repeat."

"What did I do wrong, Sergeant, sir?"

"You visited a disreputable place, unsuitable for a uniformed rifleman. And you did two things wrong. First, by visiting that type of environment in uniform. Secondly, because your uniform was worn incorrectly. Without a cap and with the tunic un-buttoned."

(Who could have informed? Small towns are a pain. Everybody looks after everyone else's busi-ness.)

"But, Sergeant..."

"No buts. And it's Sergeant, sir."

One more word and it would have been con-sidered disrespect for authority. And that would have meant expulsion. And you knew what would happen. Another year of military service in the state capital, in the famous 19th BR, the Brigade of Riflemen. There - according to what they say - any bad guy turns into a good boy.

You thought: "I've fucked things up. Farewell to my military career."

Some days earlier, during shooting practice, this same sergeant had asked you why you didn't go in for the NCO school. There was a very good one in a town called Três Corações in Minas Gerais.

"The town where Pelé was born. The same."

Well, Pelé was born there but he didn't want to be a sergeant. He went and did his service on a different field, in a different area. And now he had it all. He was a world champion.

The commander at the military training school was not just good at bawling. Now he was turning out to be a skilful enticer of youthful talents into military careers.

"You're an intelligent, educated boy. You could have a brilliant career."

"I don't think I have the vocation," you said, grateful, of course, not only for the praise, but also for the attention the sergeant was paying you, a proof that he held you in regard.

But what concerned you was something else: your shoulder, your collarbone. The kick of the rifle, the recoil from the first shot, seemed to have left you minus a piece of your body. On top of everything, you wasted the whole magazine. You didn't land a single one in the target stuck on the hillside.

"You'll learn," said the sergeant. "It's not such a mind-blower. Life in the army is not only shooting, physical training and drill, you know. It offers many alternatives. If you like I'll send for the papers. I'm sure you will pass the examination. Give the matter some thought and then tell me."

"I'll think it over, I promise."

Now you were getting a spell in the guardhouse for showing disrespect for your uniform. And to forget the NCO training school.

Fall in, Rifleman 27. Don't play around on duty.

You were close to finishing your time. All you needed was to be patient and not commit any more offences against discipline. Not do anything stupid. You learned your lesson. And the time went quickly.

The slow, precise notes of the church bell were striking six o'clock. "Six o'clock," agreed the loudspeaker service, in the voice of Augusto Calheiros, the most widely heard singer at six o'clock, over all the loudspeakers in Brazil. Six o'clock in the best up-country manner:

Evening falls, mournful and serene...

It was six o'clock by the training school clock.

His chest swelling with solemnity, the sergeant takes a moving farewell of his cadets. They had all sworn allegiance to the flag. They were ready to serve their country if called upon. In war or peace.

"Second-class reservists! Ske-dad-dle!"

The squad applauds:

"Nice one, Calunga."

The sergeant claps as well.

"Listen, if you want to commemorate in unsavoury places, go home first and change your clothes. Otherwise the sarge will have the lot of you jugged."

The boys applauded you again:

"Great, Calunga."

The sergeant called:

"Rifleman 27, come over here."

You walked over to the desk. You clicked your heels together. You saluted. Unnecessary display. Your service was over already.

The sergeant handed you an envelope.

"This is what I promised you. The papers for your enrolment."

"What enrolment?"

"For NCO school."

"Thank you very much for remembering, Sergeant. But I already have other plans."

"Don't be hasty. You could be throwing away a prize ticket."

"You see, tomorrow I'm going for a job in Salvador."

"Well, in that case... Are you going into a career with a future?"

"If there's a future for me, I'm not sure. But it's a job I think I'll like. I'm going to be a journalist. I mean, I start as a trainee."

"I hope things work out. Good luck."

"Thanks a lot, Sergeant."

"Sergeant, sir, don't forget," he laughed.

And added, still smiling:

"Sorry and all that."

You laughed too. And you thought:

"The bastard's not a bad guy after all."

After all, he'd only had a few hours in detention. A light punishment, just for the moral effect. The military training school was only a room full of desks, more like a poor village school. It didn't have a single prison cell. Those few hours went by quickly. No pain. But frankly now: was it really forbidden to go to the whorehouse in a rifleman's uniform?

Rifleman 27, that is, second-class reservist Carlos Luna Gama, alias Luna, better known as Calunga, requested permission to withdraw.

He saluted, about-faced and marched to the door.

Finding himself in the street, he stopped and waited for his colleagues, who followed him out as each took leave of the sergeant. He threw his cap in the air and jumped up to catch it as it came down again.

"Follow me if you're Brazilians. School, at-tention! Left-right, left-right. To the bar."

It was the end of a daily comradeship that had lasted nine months. Nine months of marches, exercises, drills, shooting practice, parades, reviews. For what? For a document, without which you can't obtain other documents, nor get employment. A piece of paper you need even to get a driving licence. Compulsory service that doesn't pay anyone a cent. You even have to buy your uniform yourself. But it was fun. Wasn't it though? What about all those crazy fifteen-mile marches, looking for an enemy in the woods. An "enemy" in those wilds? It had to be a joke. Left-right. Military training school: a sort of second division of the Brazilian army, doing its best to transform emaciated youths into strong men, second-class warriors. The vast majority had the greatest difficulty in learning the theory and all the instructions for the correct handling of a rifle. Left-right. Was any second-class reservist ever likely to have to use a rifle? But learning how to handle one was compulsory. And that in the era of the atom bomb.

Goodbye military training school. Life here we come.

"The war is over. Bring us another one."

"Great idea."

"Calunga, did you ever discover who informed on you?"

"I think it was the sergeant who saw me himself. He must have been prowling around hookers' row. He's a champion brothel-creeper."

"Seems he even swindled a hooker and she made a hell of a row."

"He's a great guy. The Brazilian army couldn't be better represented."

By the third round, you had already been promoted to lieutenant.

"But show respect for rank. It's Lieutenant Luna, sir. No familiarity."

"Of course, Lieutenant, sir."

"You know something? I'm sure going to miss you guys. Even the sergeant."

"Silence. Don't move. Don't talk, don't strike matches and don't smoke, so as not to attract the enemy's attention." Conceited ass, that sergeant. Must think he's some sort of hero who was with our troops in Italy, though he most likely doesn't know where Italy is. Or he's been watching too many war films. An enemy in our woods. What an idea!"

"That night march was a real bastard."

"But we didn't lose any men. All came back safe and sound."

"And heroes."

"Sure."

"Brazil's last war heroes."

"And we only took one night to finish the war."

"We're so good at war the enemy didn't show."

"Shitting themselves with fear. They legged it."

"Three cheers for the sergeant. Great commander."

"Should be made a lieutenant."

"Major."

"Captain."

"Colonel."

"Field-marshal. Hero of the Thin Dog war."

"Let's put up a statue to the sergeant."

"But first let's order another round in the bastard's honour."

"You're under arrest. For insulting a high ranking officer of the Brazilian army. A sergeant!"

"Request permission to beg pardon, Lieutenant, sir."

"Lieutenant Luna, sir. I'll have respect."

"Of course. Excuse me."

"And now we've got to find another war. Once

a hero always a hero. Our country calls us."

"Great idea. A war. A good war."

"But where? In Paraguay? In Italy?"

"In bed. Duty calls. To the whores, everybody. Come on, you guys."

"Good one, Calunga."

"But there's a snag: if any guy cheats the girls he's for the slammer."

"You're overdoing things already, commander."

"What if the sergeant turns up?"

"If he starts throwing his weight around we'll bop him one."

"Okay, commander. Let's get stewed."

And the squad of drunkards went marching off into the night, without a leader, with no war in sight, no enemy ahead, looking for a destination, in search of a future:

> *The leader of the band is here,*
> *yeh, yeh.*
> *The leader of the band is here,*
> *oh-yeh.*

You were a professional now. Already drinking like a big guy.

You left the next day.

And I stayed behind, waiting for my turn to be called up for military training. I was two years younger than you, remember?

And I was already working in your late father's shop, between classes, and occasionally I also got myself some pocket money working as proof reader for the local rag, which came out once a month with loads of pompous, esoteric articles, a high-class subliterature. What a load of bull. It hit the proof reader's ear like a brick. What a pain. And you were off to the capital city's main newspaper, that arrived every day with the evening train and quickly sold out. A reporter in the daily press. A journalist in the capital. Very elegant, eh, Calunga? You were stinking smart. You were riding high. You had everything going for you.

And who was your godfather, your patron, your protector?

A tire-fitter, who was always dressed in dirty greasy overalls and for whom no one gave a damn. Who would suppose that poor man, that illustrious unknown, that guy who was always so filthy, could wield such power? This old world's full of surprises: the tire-fitter was a member of the Communist Party. Another surprise: since when did a clandestine party, execrated by man and God, have the strength, influence and tactical power to, well, to help somebody get out of the gutter? From the moment one Party militant knew another who was in a good position somewhere. Which was the case. There was a communist in the newspaper. A name that carried weight in the editor's office and in the party. The bridge was built. You were taken on. But there was another mystery: how had you got friendly with the tire-fitter? But of course, he was the one who passed on to you that rag that came from Rio, the one you read in secret, on the quiet. It was the Party newspaper, wasn't it? You read and discussed, read and discussed, and that way you got friendly, wasn't that it? Ah, if Aunt Madalena had got wind of the company you were keeping. There'd've been one hell of a row.

> *I believe in God the Father*
> *Almighty.*
> *Deliver us, Lord,*
> *from all evil,*
> *Amen.*

Pray, Aunt Madalena. Pray that your son doesn't get blacklisted, persecuted and excommunicated.

Best foot forward, Calunga.

The tire-fitter arrived at the station dressed in an impeccable white suit. He was going to take you. Was going to push you through the doors of the big newspaper. He didn't look at all like a tire-fitter.

You'll go far, Calunga. Your star is shining. Lucky beggar.

"Thank you so much for all you are doing for my son. I don't know how to thank you," said Aunt Madalena.

"He deserves it," answered the tire-fitter, simply, without any show of false modesty. Nor pomposity.

That made your mother feel sure you were in

good hands.

What a gentleman. What a good man. What was his name again?

I didn't know.

"Write soon, send me news. Behave yourself. Look after yourself. And watch out for bad company," was what your mother, my aunt Madalena, said to you. "God go with you."

And she stood waiting for the train to leave. Her eyes were moist. She took out a handkerchief and wiped them. It was as if you were going off to the war, instead of to a city three hours away.

Onwards, comrade.

Find a good seat in the restaurant car and have a drink for me.

Dear cousin: they don't take us to the station any more. There are no more trains. We are quicker now. And we don't have time for good-byes. You caught the last train. Could you tell me, please, how long ago it went through? It was so beautiful, wasn't it? It even had a woman's name, the name of the prettiest woman in Bahia. You caught a train called Marta Rocha, not express, intercity, or some other railway name. Marta Rocha: a beauty, a Miss Brazil, nearly a Miss Universe. A beauty queen gliding over the rails, heading for the future, leaving behind a slow way of life. Really, it wasn't a train you were going away in. It was a magazine cover.

Window moving. A passing face. Slowly the images fuse. Printing presses spew out newspapers, one after another. A close-up on the front page. The image settles. An unshaven face. Tired expression. Knapsack on back, the man in the photograph is dressed in army battledress. He's a national hero. He just inaugurated Brasilia, the country's new capital. Now he needs a bath.

This time Rifleman 27, second-class reservist Carlos Luna Gama, had been called up, not for a fifteen-mile night march, but for a long march of many many days. From the capital of Bahia, over in the east, to the central plateau, way over towards the west. How many miles? You lost count. Sure, slogging it on foot through the interior of Brazil, tramping across impenetrable expanses in the age of the airplane, was not just a crazy exploit, it was a very strange way of honouring the foundation of a city. But Bahia had to be different. The country's first capital, instead of sending flowers, had sent soldiers to greet the birth of its second successor. Who went there and back safe and sound. Calunga was to be the chronicler of the event. Lieutenant-journalist, eh? Say, you sure made good. You're the greatest.

And I was crazy to know everything about your adventure. I rushed off to find you. Slumped on a bed in a cheap hotel room full of beds, with a bottle within reach, my hero was stewed.

"Now you've got to salute me, you dog. I've

been promoted. Show more respect for rank."

My hero welcomed me enthusiastically.

But fell asleep immediately.

The next night we ended up at a party.

I thought it was in his honour. It wasn't.

It was his boss's birthday.

He being not only the owner of a newspaper, but also of goodness knows how many head of cattle and goodness knows how many acres of cacao trees.

The editorial staff were present to a man.

Obviously the Great Chief had chosen a good place to live: in Barra Avenue, the select suburb on the sea front. Know ye how much costeth one square foot of terrain in a district of that ilk?

And he lived in the midst of flowers, of music, of art, of poetry.

That was a different life, I thought, remembering the smelly room in the cheap hotel where I'd spent the previous night.

Many of the good things in life, to eat and drink, were being served. On a tray.

Unbelievable: the owner of this abundance was the friend of the tire-fitter, the good, oil-stained soul who had opened the capital's door to my cousin Calunga.

The Great Chief had been a "fellow-traveller". Things from the past.

But what the devil was a "fellow-traveller" supposed to be? That strange word was not yet part of my vocabulary.

It's someone who gives dough to the Party, but stays outside, doesn't join the party ranks - Master Calunga knew his onions already.

The "fellow-travellers" were also called "water-melons": green on the outside, red on the inside.

And what about you, Calunga? Have you joined the Party yet?

No, he hadn't joined. He had already sneaked into print rooms, on nights when he was less drunk, to help make up broadsheets. He'd already helped write some pamphlets. He'd already pushed his nose into some difficult, complicated books, by Marx and Engels, Lenin and the rest. He could already say, with a degree of conceit and a very straight face, that he now knew the difference between metaphysics and dialectics, because he had by now found out that it wasn't true that there's nothing new under the sun. Dialectics proved that the sun that rose today is not the same as yesterday's, just as the shirt you're wearing now won't be the same if you wear it again tomorrow. At the very least it will be dirtier.

But despite all this he still hadn't signed his membership card. His behaviour must be under observation. And he wasn't sure if he wanted to belong to any Party either. Apart from anything else, the Communists had their differences with boozers.

"They're a lot like priests and nuns."

"But you are a 'fellow-traveller', aren't you?"

"Yes, yes. They have an ideal, they defend a just cause, they want a better world for everybody and they sacrifice a lot for it. They suffer all sorts of persecution, discrimination and prejudice. Of course I sympathise with them."

"Partly because one of them got you a job, am I right?"

He laughed.

"Now you caught me out."

The capital had a lot to teach a Backlands small-fry, a country yokel. Capitalism, communism, fellow-traveller, metaphysics, dialectics. Too many new things for a single night.

And my guide, my master, was now explaining that his boss's friendship with the tire-fitter went way back to their school days. Those things from when people are young.

Their friendship had become closer in prison.

If life had seen fit to put one in Barra Avenue, with flowers all around him, and the other at a gas station, with truck drivers, oil and burst inner-tubes around him, it didn't matter: their friendship continued.

Calunga had the proof of that.

He would never be able to forget the day when the tire-fitter, dressed in an impeccable white suit, after paying his train fare, on the most beautiful train in the world, christened with the name of the

most beautiful woman in Brazil, Marta, Marta
Rocha, the international beauty queen, after buy-
ing him a lunch, at the end of a three-hour journey, when a nervous Calunga got stuck into a very
ordinary meat stew with rice and beans so hungrily
you'd've thought he'd even have eaten a plate of
nails, after paying his fare on a city bus and then
on a crowded elevator, the renowned Lacerda elevator which lifted the Lower City in seconds to the
Upper City, and in which a frightened Calunga felt
his spine turn to ice and him fit to faint, from the
crush, the suffocating heat, the sweat, the under-
arm stink, the speed, the fear, phew!, after walking
across a square and into a street, most appro-
priately called Assistance Street, after getting into
another elevator, this time without butterflies or
fear, after stopping at the third floor, going
through a door, reaching a waiting room, where
the tire-fitter gave his name to a friendly secretary,
adding that he had arrived unexpectedly, hadn't
made an appointment because he lived a long way
away, and after noting that they were not made to
hang around in a waiting room, there was no I'm
not sure or any other shabby excuse, such as what
is it you want to see him about? He is in a meeting, he cannot see you just now, will you leave a
message? What is your telephone number? After
seeing how quick and easy it all was, because a
door had just opened and the secretary, even more
friendly than before, smiled and said:

"You can go in."

Yet, after all this, Calunga was to have even more reason to stand open-mouthed. To be sure, he did not expect the Great Man, the owner of a building, where the meeting was taking place, the owner of a newspaper, the owner of half Bahia, a state two and a half times the size of France, to greet the tire-fitter in such an affable, friendly, attentive manner.

"It's a pleasure to shake you by a hand with all its fingers and nails," said the tire-fitter.

It sounded like a joke. And, after a fashion, it was. The tire-fitter's hands had some nails missing. They'd been torn out with pliers, by the police.

"You are quite impossible," said the Great Man, embracing the tire-fitter. It was a strong, effusive, very enthusiastic embrace. "You! Been a long time, eh? To what do I owe the honour of your visit?"

"I know you're a very busy man. I don't want to take up your time."

"Don't give it another thought. One can always make space for a friend."

"That was just what I thought. That you would spare a moment. I came here to bring you this lad" - at which point the tire-fitter took Calunga by the arm and pushed him forward, face to face with the Great Man. "He needs a chance on your paper. He's a valuable young man."

Once that was said, nothing more was needed.

The Great Man straightaway picked up his

jacket, which was as impeccably white as the tire-fitter's, put it on and invited the two of them to accompany him to the editorial office. It was just across the street. But the fitter said he would be going straight back. He had to get back to his tires. In the street, he and the Great Man embraced once more. Calunga shook his hand and stammered:

"Many thanks for everything. I shall never forget you."

"Good luck," said the tire-fitter.

Man, a few moments later you'd be entering the newspaper offices through the front door, handed in by the owner himself. That's the sort of luck you need in hell!

And that's mostly what I was thinking about, that night when I was woken with the news of your death: there goes a valuable guy.

Value.

Quite a word.

But its meaning, its import, which the tire-fitter used to get you a job, to open a door for you, that's all dead now.

When it was a question of personal value, it really meant something. In the course of time, that value has been transferred from people to things.

But don't you think your destiny might have been different, Calunga, if that high school teacher had punished your pranks by making you write, a thousand times, I AM VERY VALUABLE, instead of Order and Progress?

I am very valuable.
You are very valuable.
He is very valuable.
We are very valuable.
You are very valuable.
They are very valuable.

But let's get back to the party, which was full of old and new celebrities from the world of art, culture and business.

But the most notable notable of the evening was you.

"Will you look who's here. The hero of the Long March."

"Tell us the story of the yokel again, the one who saw the soldiers in the road and started shouting like a madman, 'The war's not over! The world war's reached Brazil! Brazil's going to win the war!' "

"Then he went into his thatched hut and came running back with a poster in his hand. Nobody could begin to guess where he'd got it from. It was a very faded old poster with a picture of Marshal Henrique Teixeira Lott. The yokel waved the poster at us, shouting: 'Is Marshal Lo-ti-ti here? Has Marshal Lo-ti-ti come too?' And he was very disappointed when he found out that Marshal Lott wasn't in command."

"And the story of the SOS that had the air force

going crazy, how did that go?"

"Some joker decided to have some fun with the radio. He sent out an SOS saying the troops were lost in the woods. It caused havoc. We'd have all been put inside if they could've. But how could they arrest troops while they were marching and with a set arrival date?"

"Did the air force manage to spot you?"

"Yes. They must've been hopping mad when they discovered the SOS was a hoax."

"Tell us the truth now, Calunga. It was you, wasn't it?"

"Stop joking, fuck you. If that reaches a general's ears, I'm screwed."

To the sound of glasses clinking, between glasses of champagne, between drinks, between smiles, between claps on the back, between questions, you caught scraps of sentences coming in your direction: a trailblazer, our pioneer, eyewitness of a new History of Brazil. You didn't need asking twice: you lied shamelessly. One moment you were saying that you had at last succeeded in shaking hands with the president of the republic, and that you'd never known such a nice, ordinary, charming person as Dr Juscelino Kubitschek de Oliveira. Next moment you were saying that for the first time in your life you'd seen a president only three yards away. The truth, though, was that you were the only one of us to see him in person, at whatever distance, when he made that famous

138

speech which began: "From the solitude of this central plateau" - the speech that inaugurated Brasilia.

But you were not to be a hero for long, that night. Your stardom was short-lived. A brighter star rose aloft in the reception room, eclipsing your brightness. You felt the blow and began to flounder, burying your face in drink after drink, as you wobbled from group to group, unable to find anywhere to shelter. Even the birthday host, the owner of the house, the boss, no longer bothered to feign a smile in your direction, the ungrateful character. And you'd done everything according to the rules. Had even brought a birthday present! More than this. You'd given him the best souvenir of your Long March - the faded poster which you, you didn't explain how, had managed to grab from the hands of that yokel, the fanatical political ally of Marshal Henrique Duffles de Teixeira Lott, whom, as a tribute to the roadside bumpkin out on the Brazilian frontier, you started to call Marshal Lo-ti-ti, and for whom you were going to vote, not knowing you were wasting your vote, just as you didn't know this was to be the only time you would vote for a candidate for the Presidency of the Federal Republic of Brazil - you were to die without ever having a second opportunity to choose a representative for your country, for yourself, and this undoubtedly made some difference to your life, weighed on your carcass. But look here, cousin: do you know what the survivors of those olden times are saying about your candidate Lo-ti-ti now? Have you woken occasionally from your eternal sleep to read the *Jornal do Brasil?* Well, this paper is digging up old characters, though without the enthusiasm of that roadside yokel from whom you sneaked the poster with the marshal's picture. And the picture they're painting of him now is by no means flattering. Listen to this: "No sooner was the campaign in the streets when it became obvious that Lott, with all the nationalist fervour, the support of the left, was a weightier candidate than the Mar mountains. He was hard and intransigent, an upright man, but lacking any degree of political flexibility. Smug, too. His campaign turned into a hilarious series of idiotic episodes, like his Ceará speech recommending the dams should be covered with plastic sheeting to avoid evaporation." Hell, Calunga, couldn't you have found me a better candidate? Just look who you voted for and made me vote for too. Perhaps you'll tell me we had no choice. Even so I still suspect you were always swimming against the tide of history, the same way you were at that party. Yes, that's right: let's get back to the party. Where your heroic image lasted no time at all.

The hero of the night was called Marcel Proust.

Do you know him? Never heard of him? At least you've read one of his three thousand pages. Not a single paragraph?

Ah, Marcel, Marcel! Monsieur Proust. La Recherche. Le temps perdu. Le temps retrouvé.

Translating: suddenly, they started to talk about a monument. Splendid. Superb. Masterly. Extraordinary. Sheer genius.

The night now belonged to the clever ones. Full stop and farewell, unlettered throng.

What was the importance of a ragged Bahia-Brasilia March in comparison with the immortal work of Proust?

Le temps perdu. And us losing our time there. We were from up-country. Savages. Out of our depth.

The ex-hero of the Bahia-Brasilia march retreated into his insignificance, while the egg-heads, in perfect scholarly style, established themselves in the boss's library, in a high state of wonderment. Would anyone have the courage to ask if all those volumes, carefully arranged on the bookshelves, had been bought by the yard, just to decorate the house and impress the audience? The tactless Calunga would take that upon himself. The gaffe of the soirée. It was getting time to make an exit.

Off to the Mercado Modelo, in Cayru Square, in the lower city. Let's join forces with the last true drinkers, keep going until the last drinking joint and the last stall in the market close for the night. Tomorrow we'll wake up with swollen livers, spewing up our insides, and blaming the last piece of fried bean-cake, the last plate of calf's-foot stew or some other heavily seasoned dish we gulped down, at the ass-end of the night, somewhere between the Mercado Modelo and Castro Alves Square, in the upper city, where the poet will receive us with open arms, one pointing towards a sea of pitch at the foot of the mountain which will fall away beneath our shoes, the other at the fat old negress sitting next to a saucepan full of beans with calf's-foot, emergency rations for the last hungry wino. That is São Salvador da Bahia by night. While the city sleeps, you hear piercing sounds. Moans, groans, war cries. African hands beating the leather of an *atabaque.* While down below here, in the streets, you fart palm oil. Others snort with rage. Like old Africa there climbing a hill with a can on his shoulder.

They might at least have invited him to the party. He worked for the paper too. In the print section. No, he could never go to parties. The presses couldn't stop.

After one more night of sweated labour, he got home dying for a bath. Then his woman told him there wasn't a drop of water, not even to drink. He took the eternal can and climbed the hill. An old black with kinky white hair and thin legs. Tired and sweaty. There was a tap higher up. He bathed under the tap. Washed himself. Then filled the can. He had a wife and children. The water in the can was for drinking. He sweated a good deal on the way back. He needed another bath. Fuck it.

It'd be better to wash his soul. In rum.

He told his wife: "I'm going down the way, won't be long. There'll be a samba tonight."

When he reached the Mercado Modelo, the samba was ready, words and music written in his head. He asked if we wanted to hear it. Of course we would hear it, while we dragged him along up the hill to the upper city. The night was young and we were listening to a newly-born samba.

It went like this:

> *No one sees my despair*
> *I'm a graduate*
> *and suffering's my course.*

> *False happiness*
> *pretend smiles*
> *someone's to blame*
> *for this grief of mine.*

"Very good, pal," said Calunga. "Your samba is very good. Tomorrow, right away, I'll do a piece on you, to put in the paper. With your picture and everything. But first answer me something. Do you know who Marcel Proust is?"

"Marcel what?"

Our samba man asked leave to retire. He was going to bed.

"Marcel Proust makes people sleepy," laughed Calunga.

Good night, mister taxi driver. Pardon my asking, but do you by any chance know Marcel Proust? Say there, statue of Castro Alves, do you know anything about Marcel Proust? Greetings, Dona Maria, dispenser of calf's-foot stew. Have you heard of Marcel Proust? Salve Iemanjá, queen of the sea. Saint of mine, have you ever read any Marcel Proust? Whores, sailors, dockers, virgins, oil workers, *capoeira* dancers, railway workers, tourists, petty civil servants, landowners, gigolos, soldiers, illiterates: do you know Marcel Proust?

"Time to be moving on," he said.

"Good idea. Let's go. It'll do for today. I'm sleepy."

"Wait a bit. That calf's-foot stew didn't go down well. It's got my innards in a twist. This street food screws you up."

There was a wall between the square and a mountain which fell away out of sight, down into a pitch-black sea. Dark night. Dreadful sea. "Over your broad harbour bar has entered so much trade, so many traders." Could it have been up here that the scurrilous poet, by name Gregorio de Matos, better known as Devil's Tongue, was inspired to write those lines?

"I've just made a great discovery, Calunga. Look there. There are fireflies in the sea. "

"You drunk already? Those are boat lights. Do you know what a boat is? There's masses of them out there. You can go sailing."

"It must be great travelling by boat. Days and

nights at sea. Have you ever travelled by boat?"

"No. And stop talking about boats, I'm feeling sick."

He leaned over the wall and puked to his heart's content.

Get rid of it all, old son. Spew whatever's bothering you down the hillside. Ugh, what a ghastly face. Vomiting is very unpleasant, isn't it? Every night the same thing, he said. Drifting around late at night, with nothing to do. Just rum and calf's-foot stew. Hit me on the back, damn you. I've still got something stuck.

Rum and calf's-foot stew, a toothless samba singer and Marcel Proust, I said. Let's go home to bed. I've had enough for tonight.

And him there collapsing on the ground, almost passing out, unable to stand up:

"I know of a place where something's happening. It's called Cuba. Ever heard of it?"

"An island in the Caribbean, in Central America, surrounded on all sides by rum, rumba, bolero and cha-cha-cha. Did I pass your geography test?"

"Ten. Ten out of ten. Now tell me: where did the Americans go to piss and puke?"

"Any hole like this. But if you want to vomit again, give it hell. You don't need to go to Cuba. You don't have to go so far. There's a good thick wall right here in front of you. It's not that bearded Cuban's rampart, but it'll do."

"That's enough. Respect my rank. I'm a lieu-tenant-journalist, fuck it. Stand to attention. The beard you're referring to is Commander Fidel Castro. He and Commander Che Guevara are carrying out a revolution. They're changing the world. And you, fuck it, what are you doing?"

"Nothing. I'm only trying to tell you that there's a first-rate rampart here for you to piss and puke on to your heart's content."

"You haven't understood anything that's going on in Cuba. You don't understand anything at all. What the fuck are you doing here?"

"I came to see you. I came to talk to you. But you're drunk."

"That's great. On top of everything I have to swallow insults. Drunk, me? You're the one who's drunk. But I'll tell you a piece of news. Are you listening? I'm leaving. I'm getting out of this crappy hole."

"You going to Cuba?"

"Cuba? The hell I am. Let's leave Cuba to the beards. It's in good hands. No, I'm going south, to São Paulo. It's bloody cold there. And where it's cold, you can drink and drink and never get drunk. Isn't that the best place in the world?"

"Okay, Commander. But before you go to São Paulo, you'll have to get some sleep. You're as drunk as a fiddler's bitch."

"As drunk as the bitch that bore you."

"Don't bring my mother into this. She's been in

146

the other world for a long time, had you forgotten? Talking of which, you haven't said a word about your own mother."

"I forgot. Forget it. Give us a hand up. Help me get up, fuck you."

"Well, your mother is going strong with a conceited bloody character. I guess you'll soon be getting a stepfather. And you'll have to ask his blessing. Stepfathers are too much of a good thing, aren't they, Calunga?"

"Pull harder, man. You drunk?"

"Yup. And you're on the floor, a dead weight. Come on, get up. Did you know that your mother complains a lot, says you don't write, don't send news, don't go to see her? But she's up in the air about your success. When I showed her your photograph in the paper, she nearly fainted with the excitement. My son Calunga. The rascal. That was all she could say. And she called all the neighbours to see your picture in the paper. She says she's coming to see you one of these days. She's even ordered a new dress. She'll come dressed up to the nines. But I don't think she's going to like the stench of rum in your room. Get ready. You're in for a bawling out..."

"By the time she comes I'll be far away. C'mon. Let's take a taxi."

"To São Paulo?"

"Don't bug me, fuck it. But I'll go, I will. Just you see."

147

"Buy a ticket for an afternoon bus or you won't wake up and you'll miss it."

It's memory, not pain, that makes you remember wild deserted streets.

I must have read that in a book somewhere, can't remember which.

Nor do I remember everything that happened when I returned to that city, not just to go drinking with you or to roam the empty nights, but to try my luck. It didn't work. I still hadn't read Marcel Proust.

I reached São Paulo before you though.

Wasn't that where the whole country and half the rest of the world were making for?

Zão Zão Paulo. Big Sampa. A mass of Japanese speaking Italian with a Northeast Brazilian accent.

Great Sampa.

A heap of tall buildings facing a viaduct.

The factory. Spouting smoke from its nostrils twenty-four hours a day.

When you arrived there, it had only two-and-a-half million inhabitants.

São Paulo: the nation's locomotive. Seven days' travel from Bahia to the city's suburban railway station. When the train was not derailed.

And by now the city was getting worried about overcrowding:

"Keep São Paulo clean - kill a Bahian a day."

But I was already living in an apartment, on a twenty-third floor. That was luxury.

And nobody tried to kill you.

True, there wasn't a hotel would take you in, that first night. That was lousy. Having to spend a whole night tramping around with nowhere to sleep, tired, dusty, dirty, stinking! The very picture of a migrant worker. A bindle stiff! But you were to blame, you didn't let me know when you were arriving, neither the day nor the time. The janitor in the building where I lived wouldn't let you in either. You spent the rest of the night sitting by the entrance, nursing your suitcase, with one eye on the corner bar, waiting for it to open so that you could go and warm your bones. São Paulo did not make you very welcome. But you were to be better treated.

"I've seen all the Japanese already. Now I can go back," you said. I liked your spirit. Calunga might be frazzled but he was still witty. That was great.

"Have a bath and a sleep first. You don't want to go back to Bahia looking such a mess, do you? They won't even let you back into Mariquinha's rooming house."

"Every time I open my mouth here, I breathe smoke. Is this place fit to live in?"

It was. A few days later you got yourself a good job on a big newspaper. There was no lack of work in São Paulo.

And you were here to inaugurate a fresh cycle in your life. You win some and you lose some. Or, as your mother would say, you earn it and you throw it away.

It was like this: you would go to the newspaper offices, you would work, you would receive your salary at the end of the month and you would then disappear among the bars. So you were dismissed. When your money was at an end, you would go back into the struggle. You would get another job, and so on. And that's the way it was until the 31st March 1964, when you saw the tanks in the streets, said you were on strike and that you wouldn't go back to work any more. Nor did you. You spent the evenings in bars, the nights in brothels and the afternoons in bed reading and rereading a book called *The Warrior's Repose,* which was the story of a guy not unlike you, because he spent all his time in an apartment, drinking, drinking, drinking.

One day I asked you if you didn't get tired of doing nothing, if you didn't feel ashamed of not working in a city where everybody worked.

Answer:

"You're the knucklehead. You wake up early every day, rush off to work and when you get there you work, work, work. What for? While I'm drinking, I can feel something happening inside my head, I feel some discovery is about to take place, that I'm plumbing unsuspected depths, getting closer to a personal truth. I'm looking for the meaning of life in the bottom of a glass. Being drunk's the only way you can stand a city like this, fuck it. I don't know how you put up with it. And what's worse, what's really serious, is that you seem to like it. Go to the window and look down there. Is there any sense in that unending procession you can see, a band of fanatics blocking the streets, creating traffic jams, knocking people over, killing one another, all because of money? It's a stupid, empty, daily march. For nothing. One day I tried to go out there and someone bumped into me, nearly put my shoulder out of joint. Another time some guy ran straight into my face. Shitting hell, it hurt. Not to mention old ladies' umbrellas. You laugh in my face. Of course. You're part of the choir of contented ones, satisfied ignorance. All because you've got a shitty little job, a mediocre little salary and a pretty little middle-class girl-friend? Was that all you wanted, was it? You're nothing but a mediocrity. Just that. Mediocre."

"Let's settle this now, because I'm in a hurry. Precisely because I made a cinema date with my pretty little middle-class girlfriend and I'm already cutting it close. She's a beauty, don't you agree? Of course you do. Know something else? I'm in love with her. Isn't that marvellous? Hell, man, I can't find words to say the way I feel. In a state of grace. I guess that's about it. Do you know what love is, mister? Do you know what it is to be in love? It's the most wonderful thing in the world. Don't be sad. You can fall in love too. Everybody

151

can. Of course, you need a bit of luck to find a girl that just thinking of her gives your heart a jolt and makes it race so's you think it'll burst. The pretty little middle-class girl sent you packing, didn't she? That's hard, I know. But, if you think about it, you're a low-down prick. You tried to lay her, though you knew she was my girlfriend. That's not right, man. Stop being a bastard."

"She told you, did she?"

"What do you think? Think I wouldn't find out?"

"Will you believe me if I say I'm sorry? I was an idiot, really I was. Sheer envy. Try and understand."

"And there's another thing. We're thinking of getting married... So..."

"So I'll have to move out, is that it?"

"Precisely."

"But where shall I go?"

"I don't know. That's your business."

"Under the viaduct, there's no where else. I've already been dismissed from every single newspaper. None of them will take me on again."

"Well, try again. Good luck."

You got on a bus. To Rio.

You disappeared.

Months later, on New Year's Eve, you telephoned the pretty little middle-class girl's home and asked if I was there. I was.

"And where are you?"

"On the *Dia.*"

"The paper that oozes blood if you squeeze it?"

"That's the one. I'm bloodier than ever," you said, good-humouredly. "I'm better informed on crimes and criminals in Rio than the police themselves."

I felt sorry for you, you deserved better. Without a shadow of a doubt.

A certain São Paulo gentleman also thought his daughter deserved something better.

I lost that battle.

At first, it all seemed very stimulating, a further contribution from fate to unite us, more fuel for our fire, in which I burned and smouldered. Yes, I was in love.

(Did I mention love? Just as well Cris is asleep. She's not listening. Otherwise she'd be asking "What's this about? You never told me.")

Well, there have already been love affairs with tragic endings, and long before Romeo and Juliet. Happy endings with princesses and commoners as well. Except that my princess ended up taking a plane to Europe and I was left nursing my bleeding heart in bars. São Paulo ceased to mean anything to me, it became unbearable.

I was not just losing a girlfriend. It was also the Sunday lunches, the birthday, Christmas and New Year parties, events which had never before existed on my calendar.

There were moments when I felt confused. I didn't know who I loved most: the girl or her house. Her mother. What a momma. Thanks to her I even started to like pasta.

The solution was to move to another city. Destination: Rio. Isn't that where my cousin Calunga's living? At least I'll have someone to get stewed with.

I don't remember how I discovered your address. It might have been one of those miracles that happen occasionally when you don't know which way to turn. What I do remember is that I phoned that newspaper that oozed blood when squeezed. You didn't work there any more. Maybe it was some kind soul in the editorial section (one as bloody as mine, I wonder?) who eventually gave me a lead. All I do know is it was a Sunday and it just had to be right. You would, of course, be lying pooped out in a bed, with a hang-over from the night before's bender. Wrong. You were working. A great deal had changed in your life, apparently for the better.

To start with, you were now the father of two children, and very pretty they were too. They were still very small and were playing on the floor in the lounge. Everything in the apartment looked very modest. A sofa and two armchairs, upholstered in plastic, a small dining table with four chairs, a TV set and, in one corner, a set of shelves, properly furbished. Your wife looked a modest sort of person (I later learned she'd been a maid) and she received me with excessive affability, with a degree of affectation almost, as if she wanted to try her very best to be pleasant to the cousin you'd already spoken about.

And well.

She informed me that you were now working in television. You always came home at night, sometimes very late. But I was to make myself at home. I could wait. If I had nowhere to stay, the house was at my disposal, I could sleep on this sofa here, it's a sofa bed, look, it opens up, it's nothing special, but why spend money at a hotel?

I told her not to worry, my hotel expenses were being paid by the firm which had engaged me to work in Rio, until I found a place to live, I had a month to see to that, well, I've a few things to do, I'll drop by this evening.

And I went for a tipple at the nearest bar, to fill in time. And I wasn't sure what I liked best: whether it was breathing in the Copacabana air, right opposite the beach, or to know that my cousin had been saying nice things about me to his wife. A sign that he wasn't angry. He must have forgotten our row. After all, a fair amount of time had passed since then. Four years or so. My break with São Paulo had not been that immediate, not immediately after the break of that love affair of mine. Time was going by without my being aware of it. I was close to twenty-eight and starting all over again. It was good to be in Rio. So beautiful! After my third beer I decided I was going to like Rio a lot and that it was fine being alone and being able to change cities when I pleased, without disrupting anybody's life. Being responsible only for oneself, for a couple of pairs of shoes and trousers, a few shirts, briefs and socks, a rucksack and a sweater, a jacket for those wretched meetings, was not without its good side. The cute young lady could enjoy herself in Europe for as long as she cared, her father would see that all her accounts were paid. What was the point sending me postcards saying she missed me? Fuck it. Let her go to bed with her father's millions. I was hard up anyway. What was it Calunga used to say? A mediocre man. Attention all you mediocre characters in Rio de Janeiro: will you admit another member to the club? We are in the majority. We are the majority. United we shall win. Another beer, please. Mmmmmmmmmm. Just right.

Fair enough. But after all, love, when it's really strong, takes one's peace away.

She was not just the pretty little middle-class girl she seemed to jealous Calunga. She was beautiful. The vastness of the city, all its fortune, all São Paulo's progress, all its money, were no more than a scenario built by generations of immigrants to spotlight a love affair. To love is to exist? To be in love is to be in a state of grace.

156

I was.

All this time, there must have been a lot of things happening around me that I was not aware of. How should I be, if all my attention was riveted on a telephone on my desk, which I always hoped would ring to confirm the time and place of our next meeting?

From state of grace to state of desolation.

It was not the same sort of grief as losing one's mother, when still a child, to God, to a kingdom above all human strife.

Nor the regret at having lost those Sunday lunches in Big Sampa.

It was the certainty of being alone.

Looking at an unknown sea.

Sidewalks full of passers-by...

Please, don't send me postcards from Paris. Don't write me any more words of consolation on the back of the Eiffel Tower or the Arc de Triomphe.

Come back, come back, resplendent and white.

It would be my triumph.

Don't say goodbye.

Ne me quitte pas.

I would like to cover you in pearls of rain, brought from a place where it never rains.

And even after I'm dead, I shall dig the ground, to cover your body with gold and light.

Let me see once more the shadow of your

shade. The shadow of your hand. The shadow of your smile.

Ne me quitte pas.

And since you are there, so close to Brussels, give Jacques Brel a kiss.

He's a Belgian canary.

Think of me every time you hear him sing.

The sea's foam was white. The foam on my beer.

I just had to forget her.

"He who cannot forget his first love, will never know his last."

Let's have another.

Now in the company of the valiant Calunga.

Who, informed by telephone of my arrival, slipped out early from work. He came straight to the bar.

And that day our business was only finished at four in the morning.

I thought it was because we had lots to talk about. It wasn't. That was his routine.

Every night.

His wife must be used to it.

Something must have been wrong.

But what did I have to do with that?

If he didn't like going back home, that was his problem.

If she accepted him like that, that was her problem.

It took me some time to discover that she loved him.

And it was for real.

Whereas he behaved as if he only needed something to lean on when his legs wouldn't support his drunkenness.

She would say:

"Don't drink so much, love. You're killing yourself."

Well, that was her problem as well.

They had two children to bring up.

And she loved him.

And my problem was that I had to wake up early.

To start a new job. To start getting to know the people I was going to work with. To start getting acquainted with the clients of the press release company. To try and make them all news whether it was a ballbearing factory or a bakery. It was like getting blood out of a stone.

I had São Paulo know-how. I was no beginner.

But now I was in Rio and everything was different.

It would certainly not be very professional to start a job with rings under my eyes and my breath stinking to high heaven.

Looking up Calunga as soon as I arrived had

not been a good idea. He was diabolical. A drunken devil.

But didn't I know that already?

Wake up and sing, Calunga old friend.

It's time to get out of that coffin for a little chat.

Or to listen to the tick-tock of time passing, with no more promises or answers.

The telephone rang at four o'clock in the morning. Time for the last bar to close. Time for you to go home.

Even if only to find a woman watching at the door, ready to go running and switch on the gas stove the moment she heard your staggering steps, and then throw herself on the floor in an insincere attempt at suicide. Beside yourself, you switched off the gas and went for her with a fury such as you'd never felt before. And afterwards you slept, woke up at midday, opened a beer - hair of the dog - and followed your normal routine: from home to work, from work to the bar. Until four in the morning.

Why didn't you like going home? Why did you detest your work? Why did you, going against the opinion of millions of viewers, think television was trash? Why did you drink so much?

And why didn't I go to your funeral?

Tick-tock is not actually the sound of the heart beating. But it can be the countdown of the time

160

that heart will be able to endure.

I listen to that tick-tock in panic. When "one of ours" departs, the question remains: and me? How long?

You passed out on the back seat of a taxi, on the way to the hospital. No noise, not a moan, not a sigh. You fell asleep on a friendly shoulder: hers. Her, always her. The one you beat up once (or was it often?). The one you left twice. The one who was to stick by you for the last time.

The tick-tock cannot give back what has already been lived.

However much I try to picture you, however much I want to remember what you were like, what you thought, what you wanted from life, all that comes to mind are a few out-of-focus images.

These images:

1

"Hello."

Christ, this telephone. And now. What a pain.

"What's going on, man? What happened? Why did you disappear?"

One hand on the phone. The other fingering the keys of the typewriter. Eyes on the page with a mere five typewritten lines. This item is urgent. Urgent, urgent. URGENT. Everything is urgent. Most urgent. Afterwards you discover that there's always one more day. But this one really is urgent. No, no. It's not the news of the end of the world, not yet. The late Antônio Conselheiro, the one who dragged all that horde into the Canudos war, in the country of God and the Devil in the Land of Sun, on the Bahian border, in days when nothing was urgent, said that this old world won't get past the year 2000, but we haven't got there yet, what got here was merely the urgent task of publicising a new (fantabulous!) sandwich bar which is due to open tomorrow in Ipanema, Rio de Janeiro, Brazil. This news item has to appear tomorrow in every column in the collective hype of the most ballyhoo city on this planet. Tomorrow. Urgent. Oh, the useless haste of press releases. But who said the opening of a sandwich bar is news? Yet that's how you earn your fucking living. See you get that notice finished soon. Quickly. Urgent. And do a good job, okay? Hello, hello. Is that text ready? Hang on, it's nearly done. I'm on the phone. I'm just ringing off. The eyes move from the page to the clock: three in the afternoon. Write the notice, what a topic, a sandwich bar, and it's got to be a success, has to become the fashion, come on, Brazil, time's pressing, how's it going, finished? Submit the notice for internal approval (there's always some son of a bitch to pick holes in other people's texts), rewrite the whole thing, if required, then hand it to a secretary to be typed out all nice and neat on a ritzy IBM electric typewriter, rush it to the client, re-do it from start to

162

finish as many times as the client considers necessary (the customer is always right), hand it over for a messenger to go dashing to the editorial offices, after everything's been duly recorded, then phone the newspapers to check, to request, insist, implore that the item REALLY gets published, what gymnastics, contortions, kowtowing, blah-blah-blah, soft-soaping - but it's what pays your fucking bills. Is that notice ready? Today it's the opening of a (fantabulous, don't forget) sandwich bar, tomorrow the chicanery of a candidate for congressman or senator, next it will be an item denying that a man was found dead in a vat of Coca-Cola or attempting to prove that the lady consumer who found a piece of mouse in one of the famous Wonder Bread loaves was blackmailing the company. Yes, we do have bananas. Too much banana for my ass. But what about the notice? Hang on. I'm on the phone. An important call. Just a moment, please. I'm about to finish.

"What was it you said? Sorry, there was a guy here wanting a piece of work."

"I said that you'd disappeared. Why did you take off?"

"We disappeared, didn't we? You disappeared too."

"True. Can we meet? What the devil are you doing?"

"Working my ass off. Keeping time with Great Brazil. Sometimes I get home so bushed I've hardly got the strength to switch on the television, anaesthetise myself and switch off. The hell is I sometimes can't even gather the strength to turn the off-button. I've caught myself before now opening my eyes around four in the morning with the set still on, no image, just that funny noise it makes when the station's off the air. What about you? What's the news?"

"I went on strike three days ago. Today I'm celebrating my third day on strike."

"Strike, again? Be careful. According to the law, strikes are forbidden."

"Fuck the law. Have you seen what the weather's like? It's a beautiful afternoon. But I guess you haven't even noticed. Work, work, pal. You don't know what you're missing. If there was a Nobel Prize for the loveliest afternoon in the world, this afternoon would have to receive it."

"Great idea. Another victory for the national colours. And Brazil could boast a Nobel Prize at last. Just think what that would do for our national pride. But what about you? Where are you? Where are your strike headquarters?"

"Here at home. I'm already drinking to our Nobel Prize. This time it's Brazil's turn. What an afternoon!"

"Tell me something. What are you striking about? Against the Nobel Prize?"

"Against all prizes. Against this Great Brazil business, against all the outrageous things that are

164

going on around us. Against progress. Against National Security. Against the dictatorship. Against the thieves. There's nothing but thieves in this shit. Against the military. Against this crappy television they've taken over. It only puts out what they want it to."

"Where's the rally going to be today?"

"Right here, in my window. A rally to end all rallies. On behalf of the sun and this Nobel Prize sky. But have you heard the latest?"

Talking on the phone, with one eye on the clock. The hands are advancing. My God.

"What's the latest?"

"A rumour that's being put around concerning Marshal Lo-ti-ti."

"I'm out of touch."

"Not surprising, is it, you disappear! See'f you can't stop a bit and enjoy a lovely afternoon. It's good for your health."

"Go on, tell me."

"The story that's going the rounds says they did the disappearing trick on a grandson of the marshal's. That made the old boy fucking mad. He put on his marshal's uniform and all that: medals, decorations, the lot. He stuck a shooting iron under his bemedalled tunic and made for the barracks where his grandson was imprisoned and eliminated. On arrival, he asked who had been the duty officer on such and such a day, etc. When the officer appeared in front of him, the marshal didn't make conversation: he sent a bullet. In the forehead. They say he's under house arrest. After all a marshal is a marshal. He don't get put in the guardhouse just like that. If it's true, what I say is: the marshal has now honoured the vote I once gave him, for president of the republic."

He was already drunk, for sure. Easy on, pal. It's still only three in the afternoon.

"And you're crazy enough to keep on about a thing like that on the phone?"

"Are you afraid?"

"Of course. Who isn't? Who isn't afraid?"

"The marshal's grandson wasn't."

"But I'm not a marshal's grandson. Listen here though: do you believe that story?"

"It's as they say: every rumour has a grain of truth."

"On second thought, it's the sort of story you really want not to be untrue. But listen, we'll talk later. Right now I'm up to my eyebrows."

"Wait a minute, please. Couldn't you come here and see me? The address is...Yes, yes, I've moved house. I'm living by myself now. It's a complicated story. I'll tell you all about it afterwards. In person."

"Okay. I'll see if I can find a way of coming over, later, when I finish work. About seven o'clock, okay?"

"Couldn't you come over now? I don't feel good. Have you got the phone number of that doctor friend of yours?"

I noted down his new address and gave him the doctor's number, while my brain was doubling itself up trying to find a way out. I had to finish that goddam press release and another might turn up straight away after, how was I going to manage it? I just couldn't drop everything and go rushing off.

"What's the matter with you?"

"I'm bad, I mean it."

"Okay, okay. I'll be there in a little while. Hang on there. And call the doctor right away."

I only made it over at half past five.

And he welcomed me with a glass in his hand. Local whisky of the worst quality. And neat! No ice! Enough to make you puke! And he'd been drinking that iodine for three days non-stop. That's what I call stamina. Politely I refused a glass. The smell alone made me feel sick. He leaned against a set of shelves, still holding the glass in his hand. A broken man, yet still upright. A dishevelled man, with three days growth of beard, barefoot, dirty, a wreck. His small flat was no better: an utter and complete mess. What gives, man? What happened?

"Just look what our friend did. I called him, told him I'm not feeling good, asked him to come over, and you know what happened? He gave me the phone number of a psychiatrist and a psychoanalyst. Said I'm not in need of his services, because he's a physician. So he recommended the psychiatrist and the psychoanalyst. Said I'm in need of both of them. Dirty trick, don't you agree? What a great friend he is, eh? I only wanted him to be here, just as a friend, to talk to. I don't want to go stuffing myself with drugs, I don't want to go sticking myself inside a strait-jacket, and I'm not going to put myself in the hands of any psychoanalyst. I'm not mad."

What should I say? Let him talk, talk, talk. Only that.

And he:

"I'm all fucked up, man. Well and truly fucked up."

"Why?"

"I left my wife, came here to live alone, to see if I could...sort of...get things straightened out. I wanted to write some news articles, perhaps even put a book together. Look at that pile there. That's all material I've been gathering for years. There's a good bit of research there."

"On what?"

"It's a hell of a clutter. Forget it. I don't even want to talk about the matter now. The problem is this: I've fallen in love with this woman, crazy as a loon. But I'm really gone on her."

"What about her?"

"Feels the same way too, of course. So passionate we sometimes end up fighting. A really crazy business."

Someone at the door. He opens it. It was his wife, now the other, that's to say the one he'd left. Of course he'd called her as well. By the looks of it, he'd spent the whole afternoon drinking and phoning all and sundry.

A short while later - everything properly arranged and timed - the men in white arrived. With a written order: to take him to a hospital. A hospital case. No buts. Who sent them? The big boss at the television journalists' department, by way of the personnel department, by way of appeals from colleagues, friends and ex-wife and, possibly, from her. The one he himself reckoned was crazy. Was she coming too?

"They're not taking me. Even by force."

"It's for your own good, my love."

Her. Always her. "Don't drink so much, love. It's for your own good, love." What other woman would have such patience?

"You need a rest, need to take a rest," said one of the nurses.

He looked at me, as if asking:

"What do you think?"

I understood and answered:

"I'll come along with you."

My decision evidently had the required effect.

He took me by the arm, squeezing it and pulling me into the bedroom. The way he squeezed my arm was very unpleasant, just the way drunks do, those annoying drunks who go around hanging on

169

to people. When we were in the bedroom he started to cry.

"They're going to put me in a strait-jacket, aren't they? They'll give me electric shocks, won't they?"

"No they won't. I wouldn't let them anyway. I'll go with you, I told you I would. Come on. The nurses are waiting."

Then he put his shoes on.

We quickly slipped some clothes into a suitcase.

And we left and took the elevator and saw the ambulance stationed at the entrance to the building and the moment we got in it unleashed its sirens at Copacabana, while a radio was playing the Ave-Maria and the ambulance was requesting right of way in Copacabana's infernal traffic, then Ipanema, then Lagoa, next the Rebouças Tunnel, the hospital in question was after the tunnel, out towards Tijuca, had an arrangement with the company, would it be reliable? Perhaps it would be better, much better, than the National Health flop-houses, the paupers' beds, it was terrible, a cousin, a friend, a brother, my real brother, and not just a foster-brother, the brother who was my wellspring in Rio de Janeiro, who embodied my entire background - past, roots, accent and whatever else - in one single person, who had been the poet in the dusty square at the green and yellow festival commemorating our poor Seventh of September, who had been the real commander of the training school squad on the nightly brothel marches, who had been the *lieutenant-journalist* on the long, patriotic Bahia-Brasilia march, for whom a mother, a cousin, a place, maybe even a people had reserved their best hopes (of what?), great Calunga, now lying slumped across the back seat of the ambulance, was prodding a small window with his foot and calling for air, air, air and begging to be spared the electric shocks and the strait-jacket, while the sirens requested right of way in the late afternoon that was taking shape above the sea, the mountains, the buildings, the lagoon, the entire city, like a scenario for Paradise. He was right. It was a Nobel Prize afternoon. Despite the buildings, the traffic jams, tunnels, overpasses, sirens, barracks, tortured and torturers, and the dog-shit on the sidewalks.

We arrived. We filled in the form. And we interned him.

A doctor said he would have to spend twenty-four hours on a drip, to dry out. He would only examine him after that.

I returned the next day.

He'd hopped it already.

Wiles of the woman he said he was in love with.

She'd convinced him to quit after slipping him a joint.

And I didn't know how, where or when I would find him again.

I was sore.

He might at least have been kind enough to let me know.

2

His name appeared on the screen every night from Monday to Saturday, in the credits of the main television news program.

It also appeared during prime time one Sunday, as the author of a 'Special' with the title: LEST WE FORGET.

It was a program about Hitler.

"Excellent," I tell him on the telephone.

He stammered at the other end, embarrassed by the praise. He said: "Right, about Hitler it's okay. He's a corpse that can be flogged without problems. Still, just as well you saw it."

"Along with millions of Brazilians."

"I mean, I'm glad you read the wording, the credit title. I suspect nobody pays attention to the names that appear on the screen. The viewer's only interested in the images."

Sound and image. Tremendous visual spectacle, wow!

"Anyway, what do you expect? Television's for illiterates. The higher the degree of illiteracy, the more successful it is."

"I only wanted to tell you you did a good piece of work. And that you should be pleased with it."

"How about a drink then?"

3

He arrived without warning. He rang the bell. I opened the door.

"What's the matter? What happened?"

He slumped down on the sofa. He asked for a drink. His clothes were torn and he was covered in scratches and bite marks. With several abrasions about the body, as he himself would have written in his police reporting days. A fight. With a woman.

"She put a revolver to my head," he said. "She's going to kill me."

"She? Who's she?"

"You know, I've told you about her already."

"And why did she want to kill you?"

"Quarrel. A fight. She was up to her eyes in coke."

"And you're into that, are you?"

"No, not me. Only drink. And some grass, nothing heavy."

"I don't understand you. You only come to me when you're in a bad way."

"Well, where should I go?"

"The emergencies, the police, the psychoanalyst, whatever."

"Don't bullshit me. Don't give me that psychoanalyst crap. I knew a guy who got mixed up in that and you know what happened? He ended up throwing himself out of a tenth-floor window. It was horrible."

"But listen: why don't you take more care of yourself? You don't give a damn for your talent, for your ability. Fuck it, man, do something for yourself."

"I can't. I can't. I can't."

"Can't what?"

"Go back to that flat. She'll kill me. Can I sleep here?"

"Yes, but only tonight."

"Why only tonight?"

"Because you've got to look after yourself. You've got to get a grip on yourself."

When I woke up he'd already gone. I was left thinking it was for good this time. In a way, it was.

I knew I'd been very hard on him. I was sore at myself about that. I was hard, true, but with the best of intentions. I really meant to help him.

But did he want to be helped?

4

He was dismissed from the television station. Fantastic. He thought it was the best news he'd been given in the last ten years.

5

He disappeared. Whereabouts is old Calunga? Has he drowned in booze yet?

6

I just heard on the radio that he's still alive. He was caught in the act, beating a woman, in a Copacabana street. The two of them were taken to the police station.

7

He hasn't got another job yet. And he's burned up all his redundancy money.

8

He's gone back to his first wife. And children.

9

He's now virtually blind in one eye and walks with difficulty. He's going from bad to worse.

10

He has retired on grounds of disability. He's

now living on the pittance he gets from Welfare.

11

He's going back to Bahia. His mother is alive and still living there.

12

"He cried a lot last night," said the woman's voice on the telephone.

Her, always her. That really was love. And I'd got to miss her pork-and-beans stew that warmed up Rio's coldest Saturdays. How many winters now without her pork-and-beans stew? I'd never eat another stew like that. She was leaving too. With him, of course. Her, always her.

"He complains all the time that none of his friends come to see him. He always asks if I have news of you. I tell him no and he bursts into tears again. He says you abandoned him."

13

I found him sitting at the table with a bottle of beer in front of him.

What doctor in the world would succeed in forbidding him to drink?

He asked if I would have a drink with him.

I said no thanks.

I noticed that his legs were thinner than my arms. His trousers looked much too wide.

We sat in silence for such a long time that it seemed an eternity to me. It was a torment, to say the least.

I arranged to go and see him again three days later, the day before his departure.

I didn't go. I couldn't do it. I couldn't bear it.

"Have a good journey, Calunga. Hope everything goes well. And don't forget to give my love to Aunt Madalena. Tell her, and please don't forget, that I always think of her. If I haven't been to see her, it's not meanness. It's just that life here is the devil. You know it all, don't you? Look after yourself, Calunga, old friend. If there's still time."

14

"The communists are to blame," was what Aunt Madalena wrote me about the arrival of her beloved son, in a neat, round, backward-sloping handwriting that made me think of the old calligraphy workbooks she once bought me. Over and above her understandable sadness for her son's state when he returned - "lamentable, pitiable, you can't imagine how I cried and how I keep on crying, I just ask God what I've done to deserve this" - over and above her complaints about how ungrateful I was, never sending her a word of news, me, who she loved so very much - "like a son" - over and above the declarations of love and fond remembrances, and the complaints, complaints, complaints, she added:

"It was the communists that led your cousin astray. They got the better of him, and he stopped believing in God, became an atheist and went out of his mind. For God's sake, keep away from the communists. I'm telling you this for your own good."

15

Amen to that, Aunt Madalena.

16

He, however (the aforementioned Calunga, my cousin Carlos Luna Gama), didn't take the trouble to inform me of his return to the shelter of his mother's skirts. Were her thighs as attractive as in times gone by? Not a line. No news. Hello, hello, Calunga! How goes it, old buddy? Would you mind making your presence known?

17

Last image: a black coffin on my wall. Silent.

On second thought, it can't be him in that coffin.

If it was, he'd already have asked, without the slightest ceremony:

"Isn't there anything to drink in this fucking house? Cut the crap. Let's get down to work."

P.S.

For the deceased Calunga to read, wherever he may be (in heaven or hell, in purgatory or in the stratosphere, on Mars or somewhere beyond Bangladesh, in the starry wastes, or rotting like a long-dead stiff, beneath the ground, in a Bahia cemetery), I offer, without sugar but with affection, this lovely page of Lusitanian verse, from the hand of a certain Alexandre O'Neill, who should also be his cousin. Well, well, well.

LEAVE

To your mother the crucified ivory
to your father the least active vice
and to him who wants them
virtue's beauteous combs.

Famous words
all
and do not forget the one
that goes like this

PARENTS
what are you doing?
YOUR CHILDREN
are not small change
SQUANDER THEM QUICKLY!

Leave also the illusion that they loved
        you
to the two women over there that you
        cannot see
Only in the time when suicides
like animals could speak
was it worth shattering illusions

Leave too
what the most secret algebra
decided in your favour

The shadow you projected
someone perhaps will fix
in a cruel diamond

PPS
The End. Exit Calunga, next call. Who's next?

ERNESTO CHE GUEVARA.
(THE ONE IN THE PHOTO.)

Not you.

Kindly withdraw, if you would be so kind.

Excuse my being frank, but when you appear it means trouble.

For example: last night I went to a party at a consul's house. Hell, I didn't even remember to ask if he was Bolivian, but I know he's from one of those countries, our "hermanos". And I just had to come face to face with you there. Yes sirree: beret and all. Be a man, don't deny it, you were there. Quiet as a mouse, so discreet, one would think you were hiding from everybody. It was you in person, no use denying it. With those self-same sweet angel eyes, made to order for a memorable, legendary photo. And the same star on your beret. And so? And so I got drunk as a lord.

And I finished the night tripping over a heap of little blue coffins and black coffins.

Go away, please. That's enough trouble.

Apart from anything else, that slogan of yours, HAY QUE ENDURECERSE SIN PERDER LA TERNURA JAMÁS, is just too kitsch. And it's been cretinized to the juvenile extreme, even on lavatory doors. And it runs the risk of coming back into fashion next summer, should there be no other worthwhile topic. All that's needed is a flash revival with lots of bolero, rumba, cha-cha-cha and Argentine tango.

Take a powder, brother. Get me?

If they find out you're here, my life will be hell. To start with, the telephone won't stop ringing. Heaps of calls. A monumental pain in the ass.

● From the reporters, with their silly questions at the ready: "Don't you think, *señor,* that guerrilla warfare is outdated? And what do you think of the new Brazil?"

● From School Television (State-owned), proposing a face-to-face between you and another equally illustrious deceased: J. Edgar Hoover, founder of the FBI.

● From the Brazilian Academy of Letters, inviting you for tea, *a las cinco en punto de la tarde.* (You see? More trouble. I'm afraid those nice old fogies' memories are growing weak. That's why they mixed you up with Federico García Lorca. Pretend you didn't notice. And resign yourself to hearing forty speeches in your honour.)

● From the Globo Television Network, the biggest in Brazil and *quizás* on earth, offering you the chance of a guest appearance on *This is Your Life.* This is one you cannot refuse. A 100% audience.

● From a veritable army of celebrities, inviting

you to dinner.

●From some of our loveliest and most wonderful society belles, inviting you to sleep with them.

●From the Party, the fearless old Brazilian C.P., to tweak your ear on account of your incorrigible romanticism.

●From a kitten (*carioca,* por supuesto): "What gives with you, man?"

●From an on-duty bard, an off-the-peg poet:

hI Che.

hIgh Che.

aYe - eYe Che.

●From a middle-aged São Paulo woman: "Buy us a Cuba, love?"

●From the extreme right (keep your eyes skinned, a horse doesn't walk down stairs), threatening to throw you in the sea or the Amazon jungle from an airplane thirty thousand feet up.

●From a porn magazine, offering you a bundle for a full frontal pose.

●From a captain of industry, with the information that he has called a meeting, probably in the U.S. Chamber of Commerce, with the presence of military chiefs and Pentagon representatives, with a view to a possible immediate landing of a task-force on our coast.

●From a publicity agency, wanting to know if you're interested in a thirty second commercial for a new line of berets called "Che".

● From the extreme left, asking if you're with them.

● From a Palacio do Planalto spokesman, saying that things are looking black. You'd better split before you are extradited to hell, which you should never have left.

● From whoever turns up.

Don't dismiss the hypothesis that your presence here might be a complete fiasco. Whether for our good or bad fortune I don't know, but this is a country without a memory. It's more than likely no one remembers Ernesto Che Guevara by now. In that case, you'd be very disappointed, wouldn't you?

So: adios, muchacho.

URGENT.
DISPATCH THIS COFFIN
TO MOSCOW.

Black-faced ox,
   ox with the black face.

I guess my aunt was right:

"The communists are to blame."

Imagine the horrified face of the fervent devotee of Our Lady of Perpetual Succour. She has a crucifix in her hand and has just made the sign of the cross. The sacred gesture does not prevent her foaming with anger. Anger is a sin, Dona Madalena. Have you forgotten?

"Being communist is a sin. They're a bunch of heretics. Outrageous wretches. All enemies of God."

Steady. She's not going to say: and of their country, of the family and of private property. That mumbo jumbo is too complicated for her dear simple brain.

Did you think she would cry? No. Look closely at the expression on her face. It's hard. Aggressive. Her eyes flash with anger.

"It's enough to break your heart."

What, Dona Madalena?

"The state my son was in when he came back home. I can hardly believe what I see. It can't be true."

That's right. Who'd have thought it.

"Poor Dona Madalena. That son of hers worries her to death. She was always talking about him. He was her pride and joy. A journalist for a son. A son on television. And in Rio! In the south! And now look how things went wrong. He's come back to his mother's skirts in a pitiful state."

And she prays and appeals to God and implores all the saints in heaven and makes promises. Is she going to turn to a medicine man too? To be sure, but on the sly, because a good Catholic, brought up in the divine religion, does not mix with witch doctors, except on the quiet, in secret, but by now she would even be capable of making a pact with the devil, if she could be certain that it would save her son.

Oblivious to everything and everybody, he, her son, occasionally looks toward the house door. Impossible to guess what is going through his mind. Perhaps a question, just one:

"What time will Madam arrive?"

While he waits, he gets up, with no distress, no pity, no inner fear, no complaints. No hurry. And walks. God knows how he does it, but imagine that, he is walking, and in the direction of the kitchen. It doesn't matter how long those few steps will take him, he will get where he wants to. And he does. And he opens the refrigerator and takes out a bottle of beer, a light drink, come on, just a diuretic, don't make a fuss, quit bellyaching, stop the palaver, what was it the doctor said? Ah yes, and he opens the bottle and fills a glass and makes his way back to the sitting-room table, slowly, very slowly, why hurry? Tum-on, tum-on. Ah, great, he still has the strength to raise a glass to his mouth. He clacks his tongue. Licks his lips. Aaaaaaah!

Dona Death will be received with a toast. Chin-chin. Welcome, madam.

Can I ask you a favour, love? Thank you. Oh, I never thought you were so nice.

Well then, be so good as to explain to my mother, my lady mother, Her Excellency, the Hon Mrs Madalena Luna Gama, that her son drinks in order to forget, so as not to listen, not to hear her unending, infuriating, boring sermons. Drink until I fall into the arms of Madam Death, who will whisper to me, all loving and affectionate, full of tenderness: "Come to me, my little rogue..." So tell her, darling, please don't forget, that I drank as a form of (peaceful!) resistance against the froth of daily life. It was the best way I could find of observing time and letting it go by. It was the instinctive gesture of a plumber climbing down into the cesspool in search of an unfathomable truth. It was my struggle in the shadows. My happiness in a bottle.

"He mutters all the time. Says things no one can understand. My God."

Aunt Madalena will end up tearing all her hair out. Poor thing. A bald woman is not a pretty sight.

"It was bad company, starting with that communist who took him to the newspaper, which was a hotbed of communism. Then it was all the friends he made on the paper. All drunkards. And communists. And that right here in Bahia. Which goes to show that right from the beginning he was fated to go wrong. Lack of faith. After he went down south, things went from bad to worse. Goodness knows what he got into down there. Nothing good, that's for sure. It's like I always say: the trouble with the world is lack of religion."

Onward, Aunt Madalena.

How about one to relax? Just a little one!

"The communists are to blame."

Imagine that, and I'd never thought of that before. Seems so obvious, doesn't it? Plain as a pikestaff, I mean, plain as my bedroom wall. That's who sent the little blue coffins and the black one.

Elementary.

Aren't they the ones who put it about that 7.3% of Brazilian children die before one year of age?

That the diet of 80% of people in the Northeast is 7 points below the minimum calorie in-take?

That only 63% of the population has access to clean water? And that in the Northeast that number falls to 43%?

That there's only one doctor for every 1,700 people?

That 40% of the population is unemployed?

That almost 60% of Brazilian housing is not

connected to the public sewerage system?

That a third of the population lives in a state of malnutrition, in conditions worse than in Turkey and Egypt?

That 22 million of us are illiterate?

That, in the year of Our Lord 1986, we have 38 million people in the most abject misery?

That the country's defence budget is 1,838 billion dollars, according to 1982 estimates?

"How so? What for? Aren't we an oasis of peace and tranquillity?"

Steady on. Let me see if there's a red under my bed. I want to have the pleasure of grabbing the son of a bitch by the collar and throttling him. Let him just wait and see. He'll have to listen to me, even if I have to beat him first: "Listen here, you scum. Did you know that we already have an experimental memory chip that can store more than a million bits of information? What does it mean? High technology. Here, now and in the future. It also represents solutions for simplifying life and improving its quality. The same solutions that are transforming the earth into a new, more humane planet, where there is room for a new Brazil, full of opportunities, better for everybody. What? What will it cost? How the fuck do I know? I don't work in the Export Ministry, nor in the Treasury. I'm just a modest writer of press releases and I know about the latest advances. Hey, wait. Don't run away, you bastard. I'm going to tie you to my bed. Haven't we spent more than two decades looking for reds under our beds? Now that you're sort of legal, I want one just for myself, on a lead, like a pet dog. My own closed market.

"One communist in tomato sauce!!!"

But let's get on to the main course, Dona Madalena.

You know what, Auntie? I've been thinking, thinking, doing my nut, mulling things over in bars, bruising my elbows in life's low dives and I've come up with an idea to talk over with you. I don't know how you're going to react, all I say is don't get angry with me if you don't agree. Hell, Auntie, isn't talking the best way to understand one another? What was it? What was my idea? As follows, Auntie: aren't you prepared even to make a pact with the devil as long as he can save your son? Okay, don't worry, absolute silence. I won't let on to anybody that you're flirting with Old Nick. Well, what about our family reputation, where would that be? Once was enough, that old rumour, when they spread it around that you...forget it. Trust me, dear, the affair died right here. I heard nothing, I know nothing, full stop. Don't worry. Now, do you want to hear my idea? Take it easy. Sit down, please. Sure, we have no time to lose. But how shall I start? All right, I'll get straight to the point. What about a pact with the communists? Hold it, steady on, don't get nervous. I haven't said what it is yet. You won't let me speak. Just a moment. I'll go and get a glass of water. With sugar? Yes, you really got very nervous. There's no need to. Let me speak. Are you calmer now? Fine. Can I explain my plan? Read this and you'll understand everything. Give this paper the once-over, then we'll talk.

SOVIET DOCTORS SEEK
SOLUTIONS FOR ALCOHOLISM

Soviet society has been making vigorous efforts in the fight against alcoholism, by means of an array of socio-political, economic, educational, administrative, juridical and, especially, medical measures. It can be said that everyone in the Soviet Union is aware of the dangers of alcohol consumption, owing to the wide coverage given to the problem. The conclusions are indisputable: there is no organ of the body that is not affected by alcohol poisoning.

Nevertheless, many people think they can avoid the evils caused by drink. Sociological research carried out across the country shows that everyone condemns alcoholism, yet many believe that moderate consumption is natural, harmless and even beneficial.

Such errors are held to be the result of inadequate medical guidance and, to combat them, the Soviet Ministry of Health has devised a special anti-alcoholism program. This is a diversified program, being targeted on different population groups, taking advantage of the seven million daily medical visits for doctors to educate their patients. Health guidance clinics are also mobilised, giving talks to unions, factories and other bodies.

In order to avail itself of convincing arguments based on up-to-date scientific discoveries, the Ministry has set up departments of anti-drink propaganda. The Ministry of Health has determined that it is the professional duty of every doctor to be active in the temperance propaganda. But the main responsibility for treatment and prevention is under the aegis of the narcotics service, which consists of more than 150 dispensaries, 3500 rooms in organisations for the prevention of disease and more than 6000 emergency centres, set up directly in industrial and agricultural concerns.

The Ministry of Health will establish another 300 dispensaries in 1986, as well as increasing the network of mobile units for private, anonymous treatment, since some patients consider alcoholism to be contagious. Soviet specialists reject the view that alcoholism is an incurable or genetically conditioned disease. "No one is born an alcoholic," claims psychiatrist Georgi Morozov. He asserts that morbid alcohol consumption is due to the drink itself, which alters the biological processes of the nervous system and creates a vicious circle of dependence which is difficult to break.

Soviet doctors have been achieving success with

a special treatment. It is carried out in stages and includes methods of hemoabsorption and hemo-dialysis, which avoid serious toxic conditions, as well as psychotherapy, acupuncture, chemotherapy and physiotherapy. Patients are no longer isolated in clinics for treatment, as used to be done, but are given the opportunity of working, since work therapy produces excellent results, it having been observed that recovery is faster when the patient can change profession.

There you go again: it's communist stuff. Did I say it wasn't? What did you expect? That it was the barman on the corner, the whisky smuggler or the owner of a rum distillery who slipped this blurb under my door?

What? It might've been a member of the AA - Alcoholics Anonymous? The local parish priest? Nonsense. Rubbish. It was a big bad commie, the real McCoyski, working for something called Novapress. Damned if I know whether he's in the pay of Moscow or somebody else. Doesn't bother me. Yes, yes, the comrade who sent me this is either calling me a drunkard or trying to discredit me with our national, civil, military, ecclesiastic and business authorities. Yes, of course, this sort of thing could be a piece of more or less under-cover work by a professional colleague (a writer of press releases!), that's right, the same thing exists even on the other side, in the so-called World of

Peace. I wonder how many vodkas my red friend had to pour down the hatch before he wrote his anti-alcoholic screed? Well, but what matters is this: do you agree to putting your beloved son on a plane to Moscow? How? We'll write a letter to the Soviet embassy in Brasilia. What if the answer takes a long time? That's possible, quite possible. It's said bureaucracy's their business. Right, you have a good point. We don't yet have direct flights to Moscow. So you think it would be better, quicker, to dispatch the patient to Cleveland, USA, to the place where our generals and top executives go to get their hearts a new coil? Okay, baby. It's an idea. And a good idea could be worth a few thousand dollars.

Talking of which, how is our financial situation?

THE SHOW MUST GO ON.

And here we go:
One, two, three and away!

> ### THE CHILDREN
> *Onward comrades,*
> *to the flutter of our*
> *pardon*

"That's not right. You've got the words wrong again. It's not pardon. It's pennon. PENNON. How many times do I have to repeat it?"

> ### THE CHILDREN
> *Sorry, teacher. But what is pennon?*

"It's our flag, you imps. The national flag, you scatter-brains."

> ### THE CHILDREN
> *Y viva la Venezuela*
> *y vivan los militares*

"It's three cheers for Brazil, you ignoramuses. What mix-up is this? Schoo-ool, at-te-n-shun! Left, right, left, right, left, right. BRA-ZIL, BRA-ZIL, BRA-ZIL."

THE CHILDREN
We shall overcome the winter snows,
with faith supreme
in our hearts.

ME:
"But what's this all about, little troopers? What's the party? Have you already found the way to heaven?"

THE CHILDREN
There's no one here
to stop us...

ME:
"Stop that. Calunga. Let me sleep another five minutes, for God's sake. Go to the bar, go on. Go and see if I'm standing on the corner."

CALUNGA:
"How about one?"

ME:
"I can't."

CALUNGA:
"Why not?"

ME:
"I'm in a hurry."

CALUNGA:
"What's the hurry?"

ME:
"I'm late already."

CALUNGA:
"Hell man, just one! Hair of the dog. Quickie."

ME:
"Not today. Sorry. Keep it for another day."

CALUNGA:
"Heeee-llll!"

THE CHILDREN
Bomb. Bomb. Bomb.

The alarm has gone off.

No! Just when I was in the best part of my sleep. It's always the same. I'm going to the shower, I'm on my way. Only five more minutes. I never in my life needed five minutes so much.

Won't you ring for me again, in five minutes time? Please.

But where are the little blue coffins that were here? And the black one? Unbelievable. They've stolen my coffins. Fantastic. Criiiiiis! Didn't you see who took my coffins? It's absolutely incredible, they steal everything. They are stealing everything. Even that.

Doesn't matter though. It's summer in Rio de Janeiro, Brazil. God willing, today we shall have a Nobel Prize sun.

About the translator: John Parker took a degree in Modern Languages, followed by a PhD on the Portuguese poet Mário de Sá-Carneiro, at King's College, Cambridge. After teaching Portuguese language and literature at universities in southern Africa, he took up a post, in 1967, in the newly created Institute of Latin American Studies at the University of Glasgow, specializing in Brazilian Literature.

He has published widely on Brazilian poetry and fiction and has translated works by the Brazilian novelist Autran Dourado: *The Voices of the Dead* (1980, 1981, 1983); *Pattern for a Tapestry* (1984, 1986); and *The Bells of Agony* (1988). He has also translated Almeida Garrett's 19th-century Portuguese classic, *Travels in My Homeland* (1987).

Since 1981 Professor Parker has been teaching Stylistics, Text Linguistics and Brazilian Literature at the University of Aveiro, Portugal.